D0190736

MICHELE HAUF

has been writing for over a decade and has published historical, fantasy and paranormal romance novels. A good, strong heroine, action, adventure and a touch of romance make for her favorite kind of story. (And if it's set in France, all the better.) She lives with her family in Minnesota, and loves the four seasons, even if one of them lasts six months and can be colder than a deep freeze. You can find out more about her at www.michelehauf.com.

VIVI ANNA

A vixen at heart, Vivi Anna likes to burn up the pages with her unique brand of fantasy fiction. Whether she sets her stories in the Amazon jungle, an apocalyptic future or the otherworld city of Necropolis, Vivi always writes fast-paced action-adventure with strong, independent women who can kick some butt, and dark, delicious heroes to kill for. When Vivi isn't writing, you can find her causing a ruckus at downtown bistros, flea markets or in her own backyard.

MICHELE HAUF
AND
VIVI ANNA

WINTER KISSED

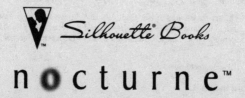

Silhouette Books

nocturne™

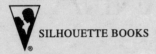

SILHOUETTE BOOKS

ISBN-13: 978-0-373-61799-9
ISBN-10:   0-373-61799-2

WINTER KISSED

Copyright © 2008 by Harlequin Books S.A.

The publisher acknowledges the copyright holders
of the individual works as follows:

A KISS OF FROST
Copyright © 2008 by Michele Hauf

ICE BOUND
Copyright © 2008 by Tawny Stokes

www.silhouettenocturne.com

Printed in U.S.A.

CONTENTS

A KISS OF FROST

Michele Hauf

Dear Reader,

So who says Nocturne heroes need to be all dark and creepy and stalk the shadows? A man who can chill you with a glance, yet warm you with his touch intrigues me. We all love Jack Frost for the fancy patterns he leaves on our windows, but did you know about his darker side? I hope you'll enjoy getting to know my version of the winter god as much as I enjoyed writing him.

I have a passion for snow! I admit that living in Minnesota all my life has made me a connoisseur of snowflakes. I can do without the cold, but seriously, I can spend hours studying snowflakes. I'd love to take up my heroine's hobby someday. Maybe I will.

Michele

To Maria Alby. Yes, we've known each other since birth, but there are still things about you that surprise me and make me smile.

Chapter 1

*"If I am too cold for human friendship—I trust
I shall not soon be too cold for natural influences.
It appears to be a law that you cannot have a
deep sympathy for both man & nature.
Those qualities which bring you near to the
one estrange you from the other."*
—H.D. Thoreau

*"Sex is like snow, you never know how many inches
you're going to get or how long it will last."*
—Unknown

After a fierce night of wind and snow, the world
awakened enchanted—a sea of glittering ice crystals.
Sun shimmered across the billowing expanse of snow

smothering the ground. Too bright to the mortal eye, the brilliance dazzled.

Vilhjalmur Frosti did not blink. Footsteps crackled as he glided along the crisp lace of ice crusting the tire ruts in the country road. In his wake, frost crystallized upon the mixture of dirt and snow.

Focused and direct, he moved through the air, alerting a mouse with his ominous chill. Formed completely of frost, he wore a human shape, instead of his usual particulated form.

He eyed the log cabin perched in a shallow valley. Smoke rose from the brick chimney, captured in cumulous puffs in the below-freezing air. The gravel road leading to the home bore a single set of tire tracks, where noxious rubber fumes yet lingered.

The industrialized mortals gave little concern toward nature, to the wildlife, why, to the very air they breathed. They were killing themselves.

They were killing this planet.

But he did not make judgments. Frost had been given his orders; he was an assassin.

Old Man Winter targeted environmental offenders, and Frost served his master accordingly. His icy touch delivered a powerful warning to those mortals who would tamper with the course of nature. If the warning were not heeded, a slow, painful death followed.

His current mark lived at the edge of the Boundary Waters Canoe Area Wilderness of northern Minnesota. Over a million acres of forest, streams, cliffs and crags, gentle hills, beaches and meadow capped the top of the state.

A whiskeyjack *whee-ahhed* deep from within the needles of a pine tree. Frost liked it here. The majority of it was pristine, if he overlooked the emissions from snowmobiles.

Stopping at the bottom of the drive before the log cabin, he leaned against a paper birch across the road from a steel mailbox. *Wilson,* read the name on the box.

The squeak of a door alerted him, and someone stepped outside the cabin. The mortal was swaddled in a hip-length winter coat. White fur edged about the neck and hem, yet it wasn't zipped closed. And the body beneath was barely clad.

A hiss of frost twinkled in the air as Vilhjalmur leaned forward to study the mark. Was that pink lace?

The tall, slender mortal strode down the drive toward the mailbox. A thin strip of pink lace hugged narrow hips and from there, the bare legs dashed forever until they disappeared into heavy buff snow boots edged by fur.

About the furred hood thick waves of vibrant hair bounced with each step. More pink lace tried to contain breasts as round as—

"A female," he murmured.

His voice would not be heard on the mortal level unless he wished it. Instead, it carried from his mouth on a dazzle of frost.

A sniff of the air detected the mortal's scent. Young, strong, he sensed no physical afflictions in her makeup. Beyond the mix of salty flesh and clothing fiber, he detected an unrecognizable sweet scent. The elusive odor teased at him.

Frost imagined dashing his tongue out to taste the tempting sweetness. But he could not consume tastes or food. No worry, smells served him all the information required to move through this mortal world.

Rarely did Frost consider the crime before he struck—but he'd never had a female mark before. What could this woman possibly have done to merit his deadly attention?

A glossy crust of ice held the mailbox door stuck. The woman tugged and then beat a fist on top the metal box. Ice crackled and fell into the snow beside her boots.

She touched the side of the metal box—laced with Frost's handiwork—and pulled back quickly. "Freezing," she muttered.

He nodded appreciatively. As if his work would be anything but cold.

"Duh. Like you expected it to be tropical this morning, Kate?"

Frost winced. How he loathed knowing their names. Didn't necessarily make the task more difficult, but, well—*Kate*. The name did land crisply in his brain, and he liked brisk, fresh, crisp things.

When she bent forward to inspect the innards of the mailbox, the coat shrugged high to expose her derriere. Pink lace edged the pale peach smoothness of her flesh as if frost hugging an exposed river stone.

Frost sucked in a breath—a cold breath, unlike the backside wiggling before him.

Mortal flesh was warm, dangerously so. He could adhere to it in his natural particulated frost state to induce frostbite. Yet a touch while he was human-shaped could transform him to mortal form, fleshed out and solid. It was an interesting state of glamour, but one he rarely employed.

He stepped forward, moving stealthily. The mortal would not see him. He blended with the snow as easily as he insinuated the elaborate frost pattern painting the cold metal box.

He was everywhere, and yet right now, he leaned over her shoulder—*Kate's* shoulder—curious about what was inside the box. The visceral scent of her invaded his particles.

She straightened quickly. The move brushed her coat sleeve against his arm. He didn't flinch; it hadn't been flesh-to-flesh contact. No danger.

A toss of her head swept shiny long hair over his face. And he felt her warmth.

Grasping his face, he pulled away his hand to find it transforming. Color radiated through his fingers. Mortal skin. It tickled across his veins, tightening, growing... not cold.

The woman turned.

Frost dashed to the snowbank and plunged in his hand, and to be safe, his face. The transformation halted. Once again, he was frost.

"Huh." She shrugged a hand through her hair and the strands caught the sunlight and flashed copper and red. "Felt like someone touched me. What a nut. Must need a visit to town, to communicate with real people for a change, instead of staring at the computer all day."

With a slap, she shut the mailbox and then shuffled back inside the house.

Frost rushed after her, his form particulating and fixing to the large paned window at the front of the house.

He observed her through the window, setting the mail on a table and slipping off the coat to toss over the back of a sofa. She wore but underthings.

Mortals did not appeal to him. They were beings who populated and contaminated this world. Sure, his handi-work delighted and intrigued them. Mortals required entertainment. He, an assassin, was loved by billions.

On occasion he did observe children building castles in the snow or sliding gleefully down a snow-packed hill. The sight touched him in a manner he couldn't ar-ticulate. But he tried not to think on it.

But no interest. Absolutely none. Detachment from emotion was keen to his survival. And mortals were nothing but masses of blithering emotions. The tragic looks their faces held when he covered their crops or carved jack-o-lanterns? Pitiful.

The woman inside the cabin stretched out her arms. The delicate pink lace drew his focus. A breath lifted her breasts, barely covered by the bits of fabric. Two points of hardness, one on each breast, fixed his stare.

"Stop it, Frost," he cautioned. "She's a mark. And you have failed."

He'd had the moment, by the mailbox, to touch her with his frosty death. And he had not. He had never disobeyed a direct order for elimination. And had no intention to do so this time.

So why the pause now?

She bent over a table, sorting through the mail. Could those breasts be as soft as they looked? If she leaned farther forward, they might spill out from the tiny bits of pink and lace.

He lusted. Often. Lust was satisfied by his frost folk—all gods had minions. But no frost faery had ever looked so inviting. So lush. As if a feast to quench an ache he could not name. Right there, in his core.

Perhaps this mark required surveillance before he completed the job.

Kate collected her mug of hot chocolate and snuggled into the easy chair before the fireplace. An hour earlier she'd hauled in three pine logs and started a blazing fire. A bright red fleece blanket wilted about her shoulders and thighs. The radiant heat stroked her bare legs.

The quick trip outside in her undies was always brisk fun in the morning.

Weird, though, the feeling she'd gotten while standing at the mailbox. As if someone had run fingers through her hair. Of course, that was ridiculous, considering she lived fifteen miles from the nearest main road and was surrounded by a good fifty acres on all sides before she saw another house or cabin. Kate communicated with moose more than men.

A glance outside was blurred by the incredible frost pattern on the window.

"That's a lot of frost." She got up to check it out.

The older single-paned window tended to collect condensation, which froze into gorgeous frost patterns. Despite the heat loss from the window, Kate was always happy for a photo opportunity.

Grabbing her digital camera, which she kept on the table near the front door for quick shots, she snapped a few dozen photos of the elaborate arabesques and filigree dancing across the window.

"Now I've begun to work, guess I'd better get bundled up and head outside."

Chapter 2

Kate sat outside, across the road from the cabin, her equipment set up near the sharp needle border of a snow-frosted blue pine.

Her microphotography setup included a digital camera, microscope objective, aperture, field lens and color filters, all securely mounted in a portable hardshell case she could lug around as a backpack.

Her work uniform was a white Arctic Cat snowsuit, Thinsulate gloves and a ski cap. Underneath, she wore thermal long underwear, a thin sweater and jeans. Layers, the only way to go.

The day was bright and brisk, a balmy twenty-two degrees—perfect temperature for capturing the larger and photogenic plate snowflakes. She could sit out here for at least an hour, snapping away, before a warming trip inside was required.

Yet no work could be done until—

It started to gently snow.

Kate tilted back her head to catch the first flakes upon her smile. Cold kisses melted and trickled over her skin.

Thrilled with her luck, she held out a chilled microscope slide to catch a few flakes. Using a small artist's paintbrush, she pressed the specimen firmly to the slide to reduce air pockets. Placing the slide immediately under the microscope and choosing red and blue color filters, she then began to snap away.

She was photographing snowflakes. Or so that is what Frost guessed after observing her strange machinations.

What did this mean? On an earth-threatening scale he couldn't determine the danger. Did she use harmful chemicals in her processing equipment? If so, it could hardly be enough to threaten more than a few square feet of air space. Nothing when compared to a giant shipping rigger dumping oil in the Atlantic Ocean and killing tens of thousands of wildlife and contaminating the water and shores.

There had to be something he was missing. Perhaps this activity was merely a foray, an aside from what she really did. Yes, he must continue to observe. Soon, the woman would reveal herself—and her evil deed—to him.

That sweet scent still lingered about her like a frothy mist of ice crystals that form after laughter in below-zero air.

Frost did not allow himself to be intrigued by mortals. Not much. The few needs he decided were emotional—lust, humor and challenge—were met by his folk.

Thinking of which, where were his frost faery underlings, his folk? He didn't sense them near, and they should be everywhere with the bright sun and the low temperatures.

He blew into the air, which produced hundreds of tiny beings, each a glint of frost sparkling in the sun.

Get to work, he mentally commanded, and then parted the heavy pine fronds to continue observation.

The woman shivered as his folk landed her shoulders and skated over her face. She rubbed a gloveless hand across her cheek, then held it there a moment.

"It's cold enough for frostbite," she muttered. "'Spose it is time to take a break."

It took her a while to pack up the elaborate camera system and hook it onto her back. Soon enough she headed for the road, her fur-trimmed boots clomping down one of the frozen tire tracks.

Ready to dash from her path, Frost saw the box balanced on top of her stack slide. In frost form, yet human shape, he dodged to catch it mid-air. But he overlunged, and caught a hand against her throat.

Something bit him. No, not a bite, but the jolting touch of mortal warmth.

They both toppled and went down in the snowbank edging the road. Boxes and equipment sank into the plush snow.

The woman let out a yelp and landed, sprawled on

her back, her body sinking in the snow. "What the hell? Where'd you come from?"

Realizing with a start the touch of her had warmed his frost to human flesh, Frost quickly worked a glamour to clothe himself in appropriate attire. Gray ski coat and leggings, hat, gloves and—cross-country skis would serve an excuse.

"Sorry," he said.

The sound of his voice, spoken in the mortal realm, and rarely used, always startled him. He cleared his throat and straightened, jamming both ski poles into the snow. "I saw your things start to fall and tried to help. Guess my skis got in the way."

With no stable surface to push off, each press of her hand into the snow sunk her in deeper. He thought of offering to help her, but the idea of touching her again put him in an awkward position. He shouldn't allow a mortal to see him like this. Yet, to dissipate to frost would startle her even more.

Finally, she rolled forward, crawled a bit, and then stood.

"Don't get many skiers down this way," she said. "Are you lost?"

"Maybe." He frowned. *Entirely too much conversation.* And yet, how else to discover her evil truth? "Is that your cabin?"

"Yes." She studied him, from the tight-fitted ski cap all the way down to his boots. The look on her face wasn't exactly accepting. Wary? The chevron arch of her brow captivated Frost.

"You've some snow on your cheek." She pointed to his face.

He touched his cheek, but felt only human flesh, which was entirely too warm for his taste.

"Maybe not. Looked like ice. Anyway! I'd suggest backtracking a couple miles and heading east." She gestured over her shoulder. "That'll take you to the trail that circles the lake. It's a beautiful trek when the sun is shining."

"Great." But he wasn't about to leave until he learned more. "First I'll help you pick up your equipment. It's the least I can do. What is all this stuff?"

"Photography equipment." She knelt and inspected the boxes, no doubt checking for damage. Then she turned and offered a gloved hand. "Kate Wilson, resident snowflakologist."

"Vilhjalmur Frosti," he offered in return.

"Now that's a Scandinavian name if I've ever heard one."

"So it is. Please call me Jal, Kate." He bent to gather the largest box from the depths of loose snow. It was surprisingly heavy, and he wondered how the delicate woman could handle the weight. "And do explain what a snowflakologist does."

"It's a self-titled profession," she said.

The smirk in her voice made him smile—slightly. Curious how her mood changes manifested as his own. He never smiled. It wasn't necessary.

"I went to school for meteorology but could never get into tornadoes and summer droughts. I'm a cold girl."

"You are?" His kind of woman.

"Yes, I mean, I prefer cool temperatures. I do research and studies and write related papers to make it all look good, but it all comes down to me, a camera and snow. I take pictures of snowflakes."

"Huh. That's all?"

"What, you think I'm crazy like the rest of my family and friends? There's nothing whatsoever wrong, eccentric or even boring about studying snowflakes. Someone has to do it."

"Perhaps so." Jal left the skis stuck in the snowbank near the road and, both arms grasping a box, walked behind Kate. "Doesn't seem all too threatening to the environment, your work."

"Why would it be?"

"Do you use harmful chemicals?"

"Nope."

"Do you raze large areas of forest to pursue your profession?"

"Nada. Are you a tree hugger, Jal?"

He matched her pace. "Can't say I've hugged any trees lately. But I am concerned for the environment."

"Well, don't worry about me. I wouldn't harm a snowflake. Er, beyond the induced melting that occurs from the lighting I use. There's bazillions of flakes to go around, so a few here and there—ah, heck. I reduce, reuse and recycle more than most."

They arrived at her front door and she held it open with a hip.

"If you'll set that box inside," she prompted.

Jal paused over the threshold. The air inside must be fifty or sixty degrees warmer than outside. Certainly he could survive warmer climes. He ventured to Florida to cling to bright, sweet oranges on occasion. Yet he'd never tested heat in this human form.

That wasn't what kept him hugging the crisp, icy kiss of winter. What stalled him was the thought that beneath the slim-fitted white snowsuit Kate wore pink lace. Maybe?

He could hope.

What are you thinking, Jal? This isn't like you. Do the job. Now's your chance.

"I don't bite," she offered, and left him standing against the open door to set her stuff down on a woven rug. "Have time for some hot chocolate before you head back out?"

"Hot chocolate?"

"Are you sure you're from this planet, Jal?"

"Of course I am. What makes you think I'm not? I know hot chocolate." Maybe. He knew chocolate; it was a sweet mortal treat. So the hot version must be…hot and sweet. Ah, so that was the scent he detected on her. "I thank you for the offer, but I shouldn't intrude."

"Got to get back to the trails?"

"Probably. Well, surely."

She took the box from him and set it aside on a table that stretched before the window. "Well, then, you'd better get going before you let all the cold air in."

Like him? Even now, as he appeared *in the flesh,* he knew his body was of chilled air, not blood or skin or hair, as she was.

He was a god. She was human.

Suddenly the differences between the two of them became incredibly painful. He located the strange ache in his core. Jal clutched his chest.

"Jal?"

"Sorry. Right. Cold air. Wouldn't want to mix with your warm. Shouldn't. Can't, really. Uh, fine then."

What was wrong with him? He didn't do conversation with humans.

"You ski this area often?" she asked.

"Probably."

She smirked and shook her head. "Well, if you get a hankering for hot chocolate, you know where to find me. Thanks for helping me with my stuff."

And the door closed on him. Jal stared at the solid wood door, but he didn't see anything because his senses were deluded with the mixture of Kate's sweetness, the dry warmth of the smoke that had clung to the corners of the room, and the intriguing fruity smell he could guess had been on her hair.

"Woman," he said. "Nice."

And though his vocabulary had taken a strange plummet, Jal could hardly care. This mission had taken a strange turn. He didn't want to kill the mark.

He wanted to learn her.

Chapter 3

Kate peered over the rim of her glasses at the computer screen. Digital shots loaded and appeared in thumbnails on the iPhoto program. She'd taken over a hundred shots this afternoon. Most would be blurry, smudged or of broken flakes. Usually only a quarter of them would prove useful.

Snow was a finicky subject. Though she'd mastered the art of capturing individual flakes, and working quickly before they began to melt under the lighting, she was a slave to nature. If a particular snowflake didn't want to be photographed, it wasn't going to happen.

She would catalog and do a data scan on her shots later.

Right now, she clicked open the first shot of the frost pattern she'd taken from the front window. At six-hundred dpi the frost pattern revealed its intricate structure, plumed and lacey and curling as if dancing across a rink.

"More detailed than a snowflake," she said with admiration. "And such elaborate designs. Jack Frost really is an artist."

She traced the computer screen, drawing her fingernail along a graceful coil that exploded into a multitude of spiky frost ferns. It was weird, but the pattern spoke to her. Like art hanging in a museum that drew the viewer to make conclusions, form ideas and feel real emotion, this frost pattern did much the same.

Of course, nature had been speaking to Kate since she was a child. She hadn't known she'd seen the world differently than others until a kid at school had laughed at her for describing a tree as pulsing with orange energy.

Snowflakes she saw in dimensions and with color, just as her micro-photographs proved.

"Sexy," she decided of the frost pattern. "And noble."

And then she laughed, because she did this so often with her snowflake pictures.

"Good thing I've secluded myself far from mankind or they'd come after me with a strait jacket. I can hear my mother now. 'You'll never meet a man wearing one of those ugly snow jackets. It has no style. It doesn't show off your curves'."

Before her death, Kate's mother had been desperate for Kate to announce she'd met *the one*. Not because she wanted grandchildren or for Kate to actually be happy. No, Claire Wilson had wanted her daughter to find a man so she would fit in, become status quo and be less odd. Perhaps a man would steer her away from that silly photography career she pursued. Snowflakes? Ufda!

"Never," Kate declared defiantly. "I love snow too much to let a man come between me and it. I am the snow queen!"

And then she shook her head at her theatrics. The childhood dream never abandoned her. One of dancing across the snowdrifts clad in a gown made of snow, and she, the queen of all snow. Snowflakes would fall from her hair and storms were lifted with her fingertips.

Yeah, it was silly, but she'd dreamed it so often there were times she couldn't avoid a wistful sigh at her un-queenlike reality.

"Good thing Mother never knew about my crazy imagination."

Yet Claire Wilson had known about Kate's strange way of seeing the world. Her parents had taken her to doctor after doctor once Kate had innocently explained she'd seen the blood flowing through the veins of a maple leaf. (She knew it wasn't blood, but that's how it had come out when she'd been six.)

It wasn't synesthesia—as a few doctors had concluded—but Kate finally settled into the diagnosis and allowed her parents to believe that, if only to stop the incessant medical visits. Synesthetes saw voices in color and heard sounds when they tasted, and various other cross-references between their five senses.

Kate saw the world with all five senses, and none of

them crossed. Everything was just *greater,* possessed more depth, shine, color and essence.

Kate was regretful she hadn't been able to give her mother the one thing she desired—pride. Even Kate's degree in science bore little weight to her mother's desire to see her fall in love.

Kate had never told her mother marriage was not important to her. Independence always topped her list.

"If I can find what I'm looking for out there amongst the snowflakes, then I'll be one rich lady, and I can build my own castle in Alaska and travel the world. And…maybe someone will finally believe me."

Because that is all she truly wanted. Someone to accept her for what she was—different, and happy for it.

With one last touch of the frost pattern on the screen, she turned off the computer and set her reading glasses aside.

The crackling fire shed the only light in the open-floorplan cabin. A narrow kitchen stretched along the west wall; the ceiling over the breakfast bar was hung with dozens of sparkling crochet snowflakes. The living room and her office space mastered the center of the cabin. And her bed sat against the east wall, two steps up from the main floor. The hearth heated the entire area so long as she kept it stoked.

Once her parents' cabin, and inherited upon their deaths, Kate loved the vast open space which still managed to be cozy and relaxing. Sure, it would be cozier with a man stretched out before the hearth, a wine goblet in hand, and a sexy glint to his smoldering eyes.

"His eyes." Kate recalled the cool, blue gaze of the skier. Like chilled indigo liquid pressed under glass. Far from smoldering, but intriguing in their own way.

"Jal? A weird name." Yet she couldn't recall the longer version he'd first given her. "Handsome, in a pale, Norse god kind of way. Lots of muscles. A little awkward with conversation though."

For a moment, standing out on the road, she could have sworn his cheek had been made of snow or frost. It had gleamed with silver and dazzling crystal, much resembling the snowflakes she photographed.

"A trick of the sun," she said, dismissing it, for no one was made of snow. And she didn't see people as she saw nature. They were plain, flesh and hair and clothing.

Standing in the doorway, vacillating whether or not to come inside, Jal had appeared starkly out of his element. She wasn't that scary, was she?

"I'm far too trusting," she admonished.

Attribute that to Minnesota nice and the small-town attitude of leaving one's door unlocked and greeting strangers with a smile. Yet a woman living alone and so far from a city—and a quick response police team— couldn't be too careful.

On the other hand, if he'd wanted to harm her, he would have done so. No, Jal Frosti was okay. Sensuous lips and eyes. Tall and noble, he'd looked like a winter warrior stalking his lands when she'd first crashed into him. Perhaps he'd been out surveying all he owned.

"Oh, Kate, you and your imagination."

With a twirl, she spun to land her bed and wrapped

herself up in a thick homemade quilt. Tonight, if dreams went well, the snow queen would meet her Norse warrior.

She was doing it again. What benign form of natural catastrophe did Old Man Winter believe Kate Wilson would cause? Harming a few snowflakes? It was beyond Jal's comprehension.

So he followed her again.

Warmer today by a few degrees, the sky was crisp and bright. Kate snow-shoed around the bank of a shallow stream, and settled her equipment in a gorge edging the iced stream. A trembling couple of gold-finches grazed the cones dangling from the fragrant pines bordering the stream.

Jal's cousin, Ice, had worked a fine job over the stream and along the hem of snow that hung thirty feet over Kate's head. Clear icicles stabbed down in a jagged spine that sparkled even in the cloud-subdued sunlight. Oblivious to his presence, she focused on the camera and her delicate six-branched subjects.

"Snow would get a kick out of this," he murmured.

Maybe. The Snow goddess had proven rather both-ersome of late. She did not welcome Jal's conversations and frequently destroyed his creations and folk with her own raging blizzards. Much more so than was necessary.

Females. Was a man supposed to ever understand the complex species? For that matter, he often wondered about the entire human race. Why was it that some were so happy and others were not?

Moments like this Jal became cautious with his thoughts. It never served to wonder too much. Yet, wonder he did.

Was it because humans had *things?* Things that appeared to make them happy? Because he'd noticed those who smiled most possessed something material.

Kate's smile intrigued him. Wonder what made her happy?

Jal moved closer, to see exactly how Kate managed to handle her delicate subjects. Her cheeks were rosy. His folk had been at work.

Sliding his palm through the air, he invoked a screen of frost, imbued with a message his folk could plainly read. *Hands off the woman.* And he blew, sending it through the air. The delivery shimmered and tinkled softly, but the tones would be understood for miles around.

Jal dashed a finger across Kate's cheek. She startled, head jutting up from her work.

Fleshed as a human, he quickly assumed mortal costume, ski poles in hand.

"Oh!" She turned and stood. "Jal, I didn't hear you come up on me. You're like a snow fox sneaking about."

"Didn't mean to startle you." He tugged off the wool cap because the warmth threatened him. A shrug of his fingers through the short, spiky hair felt strange. This human form did prove unique, if a trifle heavy. "I saw you here by yourself and thought to see what it is a snowflakologist does. You taking pictures?"

"Yep. Almost ready to call it quits for the day. My

cheeks were getting alarmingly cold, but now, they're not so bad." She pressed the back of her fingers to both cheeks. Indeed, the impending frostbite had receded.

Jal's folk always obeyed.

"I'd offer some hot chocolate—" she shook a silver thermos "—but I just drank the last drop. I like your hair."

He brushed his fingers over it again.

"It's so white, but almost silver," she said. "Nice."

Silver hair? Worked for him. But she lingered on it, as if discerning its makeup. He'd never been studied so thoroughly before. The attention twanged at the weird ache in his chest.

A diversion was required. He gestured to her equipment. "So how does all this work?"

"Oh? Sorry, I was staring. You're just so…well, you're a handsome man, Jal. Come around here, and I'll let you watch. First I capture a specimen."

She picked up a clump of loose snow from the ground and flicked a paintbrush through it.

"I work fast," she explained. "The flakes melt quickly." She slid a rectangular piece of glass within the elaborate mechanical setup. "But there. See?"

He leaned in, his cheek but a breath from hers. "That's it? Where's the picture?"

"It's all digital. I'll load them onto the computer when I get home. I've a copy of my first book in the box here…" She fished out a small hardcover the size of a pocket notebook and opened it and handed it to him. "Published last year. At the moment, I'm working on a coffee table book."

He had no idea how one would tote around a book the size of a table, but if it worked for her, it was fine with him.

Jal browsed through pictures of snowflakes set against a light blue background. The actual snow crystal appeared on the page in red, blue, yellow and clear. Interesting. But not so impressive. This was a flat picture.

"And what is your purpose in creating all these pictures? Cannot human—er, other people, like you, simply walk outside if they wish to view snow? And in three dimensions?"

"Yes, but the naked eye can't pick out such detail. Or so I've been told."

"You've been told?"

The frost blush on her cheeks deepened. "I…see the world a little differently than most. These pictures? The human eye cannot see a snowflake this vividly, but it's how I always see them. Weird, I know."

"Not weird, but interesting. So you're bringing the beauty of nature to those who cannot see it firsthand."

"Exactly. Actually, I'm on a quest."

"Tell me." This was it. She would reveal her ulterior motive and then he must act.

"Promise you won't laugh?"

If he should, the air would freeze and her cheeks would take on the frost. It would be a pity to damage the smooth, rosy flesh. "Promise."

"I'm trying to find two snowflakes alike."

Jal scoffed. "Impossible."

"Improbable, but not impossible. I've done the math. The odds of finding two identical snowflakes are astounding, but I am determined. I've a million dollars waiting for me should I be successful."

He had no idea the value of a million dollars. Her task was ridiculous, yet far from dangerous to nature. Was it possible Old Man Winter had gotten the mark wrong?

"Best of luck to you," he offered. "If it is what you are passionate about, then you should continue."

"Yes, passionate." Her lashes lowered and she smiled as she looked to the side. "Passion is good." She unzipped her jacket and tucked the book he held inside a pocket. "Whew! This feels good, the cool air." She spread her jacket wide and tilted her head back as if to cool her flesh. "Isn't the sun amazing today, even in the dead of winter?

"Sure."

"It takes a lot to impress you, doesn't it—"

The thump of darkness startled Jal. Smothering snow had thundered down from above, and crushed he and Kate into a tight, squeezing grip.

Chapter 4

As soon as the heavy, wet snow contacted Jal's human flesh, he transformed to frost. And that form made digging Kate out from the snow tricky. All effort went into focusing his energy to strengthen his crystal structure.

The heat of her wasn't helping his rescue efforts. Her body temperature melted his crystals. With a forceful breath, he drew up a thick layer of hoarfrost to cover any part of fabric, hair or flesh.

Using the sturdy structure of the hoarfrost, he formed fingers and worked at the snow. The camera and microscope, possibly broken, he set aside. And when he dug around Kate, he listened near her mouth. Still breathing. The weight of the snow had stretched the jacket off her arms, exposing too much flesh. Her lips were blue.

He attempted to lift her, but her shoulder slipped through his frost fingers.

"Cursed crystals. Jal, get it together."

Touching her cheek, a minute trace of warmth infused Jal's system with the glamour to take on human flesh—and muscle and strength.

Now he lifted Kate with ease over one shoulder. Unlike his cold ichor, blood flowed through her veins. Blood that needed to be kept warm. But how—

"Fire." What could kill him could save her.

He dashed over the loose snow. Deftly, he slid across a plank of thick ice, gliding until he landed on the road.

Jal entered through the unlocked cabin door, but paused as he caught sight of the hearth at the far end of the room. Simmering embers glowed within a pile of gray ash. He had no idea how to coax those embers to flame nor must he attempt it.

Instead, he laid Kate across the couch that sat but eight feet from the door. Cold air breezed through the open doorway. She groaned and moved a trembling hand.

"Kate, are you hurt?"

The coat flapped away from her chest. A wedge of snow fell from the crease of her elbow and landed the wood floor. Her entire body shook.

Jal tugged off her suede boots and tossed them aside. He hovered his hands over her torso. She needed a blanket, some form of insulation to keep her body heat from further escaping.

"I'm fr-freezing," she managed. "Wh-what h-happened?"

"A massive amount of snow dropped from the cliff overhanging the gorge."

Now he thought on it, it was strange something like that happened on such a cold day. On the other hand, it didn't take a large rise in temperature to loosen the crystal integrity of snow and make it unstable.

Kate rubbed a palm over her stomach. The movement lifted her red sweater and exposed bare skin.

"Wh-what are you doing, Kate?"

"Gotta warm up. I'm so cold." In proof, her teeth chattered. "Pu-please…hug me? I need your warmth."

His warmth? Not something he'd ever heard before. Was it even possible? Why, he embodied the opposite of warm.

"Jal, please."

Her shivering lips were actually blue. Should not being in this oppressively hot house serve the warmth her body required?

Trembling fingers reached for him, gripping at the dangling zipper on his ski jacket and pulling it down.

"Come here, no t-time to be modest. You were trapped in the snow, t-too. Body heat is the best cure for hypothermia."

Not if the man you're hugging is the master of frost-bite.

But while Jal's mind protested, his glamorized human body leaned in and allowed whatever was about to happen…happen.

"Don't worry," her words trembled out. "I trust you. You rescued me, so I believe you don't wish me harm."

"Harm? No." Not at this moment.

Kate's arms slid around his body. The searing heat of her startled him. He flinched, but then the novelty of the moment settled his anxiety.

He pulled her close and she wrapped her legs around his hips and her torso snugged firmly against his. The sensation of woman and the sweet smell of her overwhelmed any apprehension to her body heat. The clothing between them did little to disguise the curves of her breasts, the hard plane of her stomach. The squeeze of her legs, drawing him closer, demonstrated desperate want for…

This human wanted? Yes, warmth. It would make her happy. And he realized, for the first time, that different situations required different means to happiness. Interesting.

Tentative, Jal nuzzled his nose into Kate's hair. The cool strands were slick and soft, like a fine fabric the Summer gods would value highly.

Mercy, what was this? He felt so…

Well. He *felt*.

Was this what happiness felt like?

"Oh, that's good." The shiver had left her voice; now it was deep, whispery.

"Good? So this…makes you happy?"

"Yes. Warmth is happiness." A hand slid up and down his back beneath the jacket and against a shirt thinner than Ice's finest creations. "You're pretty cold yourself. But I'll warm you up."

"Sure. Uh…"

"Thank you for getting us out, Jal," she said, her breath hot against the base of his neck. "That was the freakiest thing. Like a mini avalanche. Things like that don't happen in Minnesota."

No, they did not. And no amount of sensory overload could erase the disturbing thought from his mind. Had Snow purposefully intervened? Why?

"I have this weird ability to survive freak accidents," Kate muttered. "Like my parents."

The warmth of her gushed over his neck, permeating deeply. How could breath feel so luscious? "Oh?"

"Yes, but they're gone now. Three times a charm, but the fourth? Deadly. So! Nice way to get to know a person, eh?"

He peered down into eyes the color of new grass. It was as if he held a piece of spring—and spring was never his favorite season. Yet if it was appealing as Kate's eyes perhaps he'd overlooked the value of the season.

"Jal? What's wrong? Are you getting warmer? You still look so cold."

Was he getting warm? Not a good thing. And yet, what he did next would surely be his undoing.

Leaning in, Jal brushed his lips across Kate's mouth. Her soft skin tickled his. Millions of tiny light beams sparkled through his system. The minute touch spread through his shoulders and arms, down his torso and legs, to his very toes. He wagered the sensation even entered his ichor, for all of him seemed to effervesce.

He knew what a kiss was. If he wished to sate his carnal desires, he chose a frost faery to service him.

But Kate Wilson was not made of frost, nor did she chill him to a tremulous and satisfying climax. She…stirred him. She made him feel things he'd never experienced. Warmth. Wonder. Perplexity.

Happiness?

Asking a complete stranger to hug her was about the most forward thing Kate had ever done. But it had been medical necessity, a matter of survival.

Okay, so she hadn't been knocking on death's door—but still.

And he had been the one to kiss first.

Now Kate wrapped her arms around Jal's wide shoulders and climbed onto his lap as he knelt before the sofa. His perfect mouth explored her lips carefully, not too insistently. The gentle approach fired her desire.

Two years ago, her friends had all laughed when she'd announced she was packing up and moving to her parents' cabin. So far from civilization, they'd whined. And men! There were no men up there, save for rednecks and outdoorsmen.

Kate hadn't missed anything that a vibrator couldn't take care of.

Until now. She'd missed the contact, two bodies discovering one another. The delicious giddiness of the first kiss.

Crushing her mouth over Jal's, she fit her body to his hard, muscled chest. Her nipples jutted beneath the sweater. She crushed her breasts to him, wanting him to know how much he turned her on.

She glided her fingers through his silver hair, noting it was cool as pine needles. He did not warm as quickly as she had. Hell, fire flooded her veins on licking torrents. This man could bottle his heat, sell it as emergency frostbite cure and make a fortune.

"Kate." One finger flicked her nipple through the sweater, but it hadn't been intentional. In fact, he flinched away at that touch. There was something innately innocent about the man, and yet, he was strong and brut as the warrior she'd first imagined him to be. "You're so hot, Kate."

Blowing stray strands of hair from her face, Kate smiled at his curiously stunned expression. "Thanks. I try."

"Maybe a little too hot." He pushed her up onto the couch and stumbled backward, catching himself as he tripped over the ottoman behind his legs. "I should be going. Your equipment!" He shrugged down the sleeves of his coat and blew out a huff, as if sweating. And he likely was. He'd certainly turned up her thermostat. "Gotta go!"

Never had a man dashed from her arms. Kate could but sit, stunned, as she watched Jal high-tail it out of her cabin and slam the door behind him.

"Huh." She toed the fur rimming one of her boots. "I thought the kiss was pretty good, myself. What's his deal?"

As soon as Jal hit the snow his body transformed and the glamour of mortal clothing slipped away. In particulated frost form, he raced through the air, the brisk chill reviving and sharpening his soggy instincts.

He'd kissed the girl!

An exquisite, hot, mortal woman whom he had been sent to assassinate for reasons that still eluded him.

What had become of Vilhjalmur Frosti, the cold, emotionless assassin? He wasn't using logic, he was…he was thinking far too much. Thinking about humans and their quest for happiness. Following the strange ache in his chest until it had led him to Kate.

By all the snows, that had been superb contact. Flesh to flesh. The infusion of her heat had scurried through him, exciting parts of him and awakening a stirring he still felt in his groin even though he wasn't in human form.

"You're being foolish," he chided as he landed the camera equipment and flaked across the metal into frost.

Breathing out frost crystals, he summoned myriads of folk. The miniscule crystals attached to the camera and equipment and soon it was lifted into the air. The entire assembly swiftly made way to the stoop before Kate's cabin.

Dismissing his folk with a sigh of gratitude, Jal, still of frost, formed human shape, then stepped to the front window and breathed over the glass. Curls and arabesques formed a grand design. It was all he could offer.

Chapter 5

Kate sat upright, instantly awake, which she attributed to her inner clock being averse to lingering in bed. In the bathroom, she splashed her face with water. An exaggerated shiver had her bouncing down the hall to adjust the furnace up a degree. The temperature had dropped noticeably overnight.

Stepping into her boots, she then shrugged on her coat, without zipping it but instead tugging it tightly closed, to trek outside and around back of the cabin for firewood.

She found her camera and equipment on the front step. A cursory check couldn't determine how badly things might have been damaged, but it would certainly set back her quest.

Setting the equipment inside the house, she then

glimpsed the glint of morning sun against a bizarre coating of frost on the front window.

"Wow, that's just…it covers the entire window."

Boots crunching across the compacted snow, she approached the glass, marveling at the artwork. Normally frost clung to a corner, not the entire window.

Stepping back, Kate realized the frost pattern became less a frenzied mix of sharp dashes and coiling curls. It seemed to spell something…in reverse.

"Sorry?" Kate blinked. No, she couldn't be seeing things right. "I am not a pig and spiders do not come out in the wintertime. It's your imagination, Kate."

She went back inside, forgetting about the firewood, and trying to forget the window—but she couldn't resist a glance over her shoulder. The word read in the obverse now. It really did say *Sorry*.

"Not dreaming. But maybe touching insanity."

Instead of taking a picture, Kate searched for the red plastic ice scraper and found it under a glove by the door. Racing outside, she stroked frantically across the glass until her face was covered with melting frost crystals and water dribbled down her chin.

"You are not going insane, you are not going insane," she declared loudly. Turning, she found Jal sitting on her front step.

"I am going insane," she muttered, clutching her stomach and wielding the ice scraper weapon-like before her. "How do you do that? Always appearing out of nowhere? Skiing so early?"

The silver ski suit made him a fashion model fresh

from the pages of *Vogue*. No jacket or gloves, not even a cap for his silver hair. The Nordic warrior had transformed to some kind of ice god. Had he not flesh he would have blended into the surroundings.

And yet, today his eyes sparkled as if ice. They had depth, and colors glinted within the crystal orbs much as icicles hanging from a rain gutter did.

She was seeing things that weren't there again. Only nature appeared so vivid and fathomless, humans were plain.

Yeah, keep repeating that, Kate. He's plain. He's not different or intriguing, or, hell, sexy.

Had she just kissed him yesterday? Yes, and she'd do it again if he let her.

"I couldn't stay away," he said, drawing her attention from his crystal eyes. "Why did you scrape off the frost? Don't you find it pretty?"

"I do." She looked at her handiwork. Long scrapes obliterated the clingy frost. "I just…it covered the entire window. I couldn't see out."

Yeah, and pigs do not talk to spiders. Just keep a cool head, Kate. "It is pretty, the frost. It speaks to me."

"Really?" He stood, propping a hand on the ski he'd stuck into the snow bank. Could a man get more good-looking? Forget *Vogue,* he was *Men's Health* cover material with a blurb line promising killer abs by utilizing a cross-country ski regimen. "What does it say to you?"

"It says beware men who run from my kisses." Right, Kate. Be smart. Living alone in the middle of nowhere.

Flick on your stalker radar, and pay attention. "I should go inside."

"Does it offer any warnings about women romping about in their underthings in eighteen degree weather?"

"It's not eighteen degrees. It must be close to thirty. It's a beautiful day."

"It's eighteen there in the shade of your house. And you're going to catch a chill soon if you don't zip up that coat."

Oh, yeah? So Mister Fashion Model was going all Doctor Chicken Soup on her? She *should* zip up. She wore a camisole and panties, and it was cold. But looking at Jal warmed her by ten degrees.

"I don't know where you come from or what your deal is." She stepped up to him, her boots crunching the snow like Styrofoam and stroked a finger down the sleek smooth silver fabric. He should talk. His jacket was unzipped and it revealed a thin blue sweater to match his icicle blue eyes. "But you're here, and you intrigue me."

"Like your snowflakes?"

"Yes, they all appear similar at first glance, but when you really study them, and see the makeup of each individual flake, you discover something truly wonderful."

Jal looked down and to the side. Shy? Well, she had a cure for that.

Kate tilted up on tiptoes to meet his mouth. His lips were cold, but so were hers. "You think I'm too hot for you? Am I cold enough now?"

"Cold enough," he murmured and then made the kiss his own.

Wintergreen coolness and Sunday afternoon snow slides filled Kate's thoughts as she indulged in the kiss. One reason she loved winter so much were the many ways a woman could warm up. Snuggled up to a handsome stranger. Breathing his cool breath. Drawing in his air, which tickled the back of her throat with the brisk bite of winter.

His flesh was cold, as icy as the skiwear looked. Yet, the coolness of him proved more exotic than a tropical vacation beach. Were she a snow goddess she would crown this man her snow king.

"So tell me more about yourself," she said, forcing herself up from the kiss. The back of her throat felt sore, as if she'd swallowed tiny ice shards. Could a cold be coming on?

"Do you really need to know?" He kissed her jaw, and glided snowflake kisses down her neck.

"Not really." Her nipples were harder than rime on steel. Jal landed on them with soft, nuzzling caresses from his mouth. "Oh, yes, that's…yes."

She lost her balance and, feeling herself fall, tugged Jal down with her. They landed the snow bank before her front window. Kate's jacket splayed wide, and the crisp skitter of snow crystals tickled her bare thighs and throat. But she didn't feel the cold. Not with Jal's mouth moving down her stomach to nibble at the lacy hem of her camisole.

He swished snow across her abdomen, and followed with hard kisses, and then lighter, tickling ones that licked away the droplets. Kate giggled and slid her fingers through his cool, short hair. She moaned sweetly as his explorations landed on her lace panties.

He breathed upon her mons, a chilly touch that made her shiver.

"Very hot," he said. "You tempt me beyond my safe zone, Kate Wilson."

"You have a safe zone?" Spreading out her arms, her fingers dug into the snow and the packed crystal flakes melted against her palm. "I thought only women were concerned about stuff like that. I don't have any zones I want to keep you away from."

"Be that as it may."

He'd journeyed back up to her lips, which was a little disappointing. But then really, what did she expect on their first makeout session?

"The speed of my attraction to you cautions me," he explained.

"You like to take things slow?"

"I'm not sure. Do you?"

"Slow is better for someone you hardly know. This is good, lying here in the snow."

"Does it make you happy?"

"It does, in a slightly twisted wouldn't-this-be-much-better-inside kind of way."

"Your cheeks." He touched one and then the other. "You'd best get inside."

"Only if you'll come with me. And promise not to run."

He drew in a heavy breath. "Can't do that. I have…work to do."

"You work around here? In the Boundary Waters?"

"Yes. Er…surveying."

Surveying all his lands. A grand fantasy she'd formed upon initially bumping into him but probably more like surveying specific trees or landmarks for the local DNR office.

"Can you come back after your work is finished?"

"I'd like that." His hair prickled her cheek as he leaned in to whisper against her ear. "A kiss to keep me in your thoughts."

This kiss crackled brightly upon her mouth. Winter frost to springtime. Yet again, at the back of her throat, the ice of his breath scratched.

Jal left swiftly again. Grasping her throat, Kate sat up and watched as he wandered down the road, skis slung over one shoulder. Whistling.

A glitter of frost crystals misted in his wake. The myriad colors dazzled. Probably snow stirred up by the wind as he briskly passed. Except, it wasn't windy.

"To do survey work?" Kate tugged her coat tight across her stomach. "There's something strange about that man. But whatever it is, I don't want to know."

Stupid, she knew. Maybe it was the childhood snow queen inside of her that wanted this fantasy to be real. More likely, it was the cool prickle of Jal's kiss lingering on her lips.

"Why?" Jal asked as he paced before the great and mighty Old Man Winter. "I need a reason for this job."

"You've never required a reason before," sounded in Jal's head.

Old Man Winter did not so much speak as rumble his thoughts through the air. The god was without form and appeared to Jal as a brilliant whiteness and so cold. He liked the feeling of strength and utter domination the winter god possessed. And he feared it.

"True, I never question my orders. You have always sent me after the deserving, those mortals who will never understand, who must be removed from the food chain before they cause great harm. I've been busy of late."

"You do fine work."

Jal shimmered brightly to show deference to his master. Humans considered him a mere artist, creator of frilly frost patterns. Old Man Winter offered him the respect his work deserved.

"Kate Wilson threatens no part of the natural world I can figure," Jal said. "She spends her days photographing snowflakes. I can only imagine her images, when presented to the world, would *increase* an awareness for the beauty of nature and not harm it."

"Enough! If you think to disobey an order, than I shall see to crushing you, Vilhjalmur Frosti, and wiping this world free of your presence."

Jal shuddered, his essence crackling smartly. "No, no, I—it will be done. Well met, Old Man Winter. I leave you with all respects."

And he shimmered away from Nordika, entering the mortal realm at the North Pole where all time zones were accessible with but a step. There was work to be done, frost folk to be dispatched throughout the Northern hemisphere.

But instead of ensuring the world was covered with frost, Jal ruminated on something Kate had said after he'd warmed her following the avalanche.

I have a weird ability to survive freak accidents, my parents, too.

How many times had she been destined to perish, only to survive? Surely one so strong was meant to be in this world. She practiced a benign profession. And her goal? To find two snowflakes the same. Impossible. No mortal being could ever catalog all the snowflakes in the world. And Jal knew she would never find duplicates.

Kate would harm none.

But he could not disobey Old Man Winter.

He needed irrefutable proof, though, before he ended the life of one of winter's most stunning inhabitants.

Chapter 6

The database Kate had designed to compare snowflake photos ran them through dozens of comparison checks, using a mathematical equation to delineate the various branches, spikes, dendrites and columnar structures. There was a surprising variety of basic snowflake shapes, and this program put each photo through the rigors. It was a long process and worked through the night on Kate's daily photographs, producing a printed report by the morning.

Looking over the printout assessed the usual results. Still no luck. But she was determined.

Two snowflakes alike? The mathematical possibilities ruled out the minutest potential. If ever she were to find a match it would probably be one of the hexagonal plate types of flakes. They possessed but a length and width and were simple crystals that looked like a tiny clear hexagon.

The idea of finding matches had always intrigued Kate. It was an obsession.

Surely as a child growing up in rural Minnesota who spent her days outside digging in the white stuff, making forts, sliding, snowballing and snowmobiling, she hadn't any choice but to like snow. It was marvelous. It was delicate, gorgeous and breathtaking. It was not the flat white star design that most believed, but snow had depth, color and intensity. At the same time it could be dangerous, angry and life stealing, as she had learned yesterday.

And Kate wanted to master it.

When a physics professor from her alma mater, the University of Minnesota, had offered her a million dollars to find a match, she'd taken the challenge.

It fueled Kate's blood to master a challenge. She'd graduated from the university two years ago. With a BS in Science and a Masters in meteorology, she had initially toyed with the idea of being weather girl for a local television station. She could do the fake smile, yet the long hours and her lack of interest in summertime weather, had nixed that plan.

A million dollars could buy some land in Alaska and allow her to travel the world's Arctic landscapes, further increasing her photographic portfolio. She didn't need fame, but she did like her independence. Money could make a woman very independent.

Setting aside the printout, she browsed the photograph thumbnails.

"If snow had a personality," she muttered as she looked over one of the pictures from yesterday's shots, "it would be a sexy young woman with a vengeance for an ex-boyfriend. Teasing, playful and alluring, but don't mess with me, mister."

Kate smiled and glanced to the frost-free front window. "As for frost? I think he'd be rather secretive, a little arrogant and icy cool."

The touch of Jal's kiss tickled a shiver of remembrance up her spine. "Yes, a lot like him."

"Hey, Snow, long time no talk."

Jal wandered the elaborate quarters Snow kept in Nordika, where the winter gods resided. Unlike his own home of ice and frost, Snow's home resembled a mortal's residence with paneled wood walls and thick, cozy sofas and even a fake fireplace at the end of the massive room.

"Frost," the Snow goddess acknowledged. She did not look up from her focus on what looked like a wool scarf fashioned from red yarn.

"How's things?" he asked, unsure how to approach the goddess with the real question. She'd been cranky lately. And yet, he had never been one to avoid seeking truth. "Crush any mortals beneath avalanches lately?"

"If only," she said, and sighed out a cloud of flakes.

"How about crushing them beneath minor drops of snow in gorges that shouldn't normally see such an accident?"

Snow spun around, arms crossed over her chest. Her

long white hair crackled and mists of snow furled out from the strands. She wore a human shape—all of snow—just as Jal focused his form to resemble a human shape, yet he remained all of frost.

Snow smirked. "She dead?"

"Kate Wilson? No, I dug her out."

"Look at you." She strolled past him. "Playing with the humans. What were you trying to prove with that heroic rescue, Frost? That you're better than me? You know you're not."

"I…hmm." Technically he did rank lower than Snow. She was right below Old Man Winter, followed by him and Ice, who were equals. "Why do you think Old Man Winter ordered the hit on her?"

She shrugged. Snow glittered from her shoulders and piled at Jal's frost feet.

Her silence raised his suspicions.

"Old Man Winter didn't order the hit, did he?"

A snow brow arched wickedly above her eye. "Of course he did."

Right, but Snow had her fingers in the brew, he felt sure. "Old Man Winter ordered the hit. Yet when I couldn't do it, you thought to take matters in hand."

"You're very perceptive, Frost. I guess that ends this conversation. Good seeing you. Ta."

"Not so fast." He gripped her by the throat. Frost hardened the crystal structure of her snow. She cracked out a wheeze. "What are you up to, Snow? Kate Wilson is not deserving. She is of no concern to nature."

"She is."

Blasted in the face with a storm of flakes, Jal released Snow's neck and choked on the swallowed litter of snow. So she was going to play things the hard way?

"Looking a bit melty around the cheeks, eh, Snow?"

She delivered him an icy glare.

"I can fix that for you." He blew frost crystals at her, and her cheeks hardened to rough rubble of rime.

Snow couldn't move her jaw, yet rage exploded from her in a storm that swept the room and swirled about Jal. He was accustomed to snowstorms, but not his own personal blizzard. Pummeled in the chest, he took the weight of the goddess's anger. Limbs splaying, he stumbled backward.

"Two snowflakes alike?" she growled. "What does she think she's doing? Do you know how that makes *me* feel?"

"You feel nothing!"

"I feel—" The Snow goddess snapped up and stomped away.

"It'll never happen." Spitting at the snow that poured over his face, he struggled not to swallow it.

"Of course it won't." She reformed ten feet away. All of snow, yet shaped as a gorgeous female, she had never attracted Jal beyond respect and admiration for the beauty she created. "But the humiliation of what she's doing must not go unpunished."

"So you want to kill this woman because you feel threatened by something you know will never occur?"

How *did* the female mind work? Their mysterious behavior baffled him.

"There's got to be something more," he urged. "Kate's

offense to you is not worthy of death when compared to a deforestation crew plowing down thousands of acres of rain forest to make superfluous products for demanding consumers."

"I've never known you to be judgmental, Frost. What's up with that?"

Yes, what had happened that he was so quick to defend one human over another? This wasn't him. He didn't care.

Did he?

"Regarding this particular mark," Snow warned, "I'll be the one to decide the worthiness of offense."

"You've no right!"

What to say? How to pry out what he sensed lurked within the goddess beneath the surface of her hard snowpack exterior.

"Your work is splendid," he offered, tempering the sly tone in his voice. "Always much finer and more gorgeous than anything myself or Ice could ever produce."

"Naturally." She flipped back a storm of hair over a shoulder and picked up the scarf from the back of the brown velvet sofa.

"Did you make that?" he tried. "It's for warmth, isn't it?"

"It is." She toyed with the fringed hem of the object, a bit too concerned over a mortal product designed to prevent the chill of snow.

Snow paced across the room, which took her far from Jal in but a few seconds, and then as quickly, back to his side.

Snowflakes sifted about her as she bowed her head. "Have you ever been in love, Jal?"

Love? He'd heard the word. "Why do you ask?"

That she shrugged again struck him deeply. So human the goddess's gestures. It disturbed him to wonder at her actions.

Love? It was something similar to lust, but emotion-based.

"Doesn't matter," she finally said. "But I will tell you this. *She* was supposed to be the next Snow goddess."

"She? Who?" And then he instinctually knew. "But… are you sure? Why then would you seek to destroy her?"

"Jal, you forget your younger years as your time draws near."

Indeed. Gods did not measure time with days, weeks or hours. And yet, each of the winter gods served a short service to the world. But his memory failed him as to length.

"Every thousand mortal years," Snow began, "a chosen changeling child is born in the mortal realm and instantly orphaned. As we were when you and I were born. The gods then take that child into their care and train him or her to replace the current Snow or Ice or Frost."

"Yet it seems I spent some time as the former Frost's folk…"

"You did. You don't recall much of that servitude. It would destroy you were you to have recall of such menial labor."

Yes, and a short span of existence, as well. His frost

folk generally survived the trip to the mortal realm, did their deed, then evaporated or melted.

"So Kate was to be the next Snow goddess?"

"Yes, but something went wrong. She wasn't orphaned following her birth. Not even after the Universe attempted to kill off her parents three times."

"She did…" Jal stopped his confession…*mention something like that.* That she and her parents had survived freak accidents. "So what does that mean? Why kill her now?"

"Because!" An explosion of snow surrounded the goddess at her outburst, settling to drifts about her ankles. "I am bored of this job, and now I must wait another thousand years for another changeling to be born. I cannot *conceive* another thousand years. I'm ready for the mortality granted me when I step down from my servitude. I want to be human, Frost."

Human? A strange desire. A concept he could not quite comprehend. And yet, touching a human was marvelous.

"And you think killing Kate Wilson will clear the way for a new Snow goddess to be born?"

"Yes."

"Have you proof?"

"No, but it makes sense."

"I won't allow it."

"Why? Are you in love with the human? You are." Her eyes glittered with perfectly formed snowflakes, a disconcerting dazzle Frost had to look away from or become enchanted.

"I don't know what love is," he murmured quietly.

"You do, you just don't realize it yet."

Jal opened his mouth to reply, but instead looked aside, crimping his brow. He wasn't sure what he knew, actually. What Snow had said…he had been born to the mortal realm?

"Love or not, she needs to go," Snow snapped. "That's all there's to it. And so what if my folk have been making copies of flakes? It's not worth the effort relentlessly crafting new ones. I tell you, there's only so many ways to shape a snowflake."

"You *are* making copies. So then—" If Kate were diligent her research could be successful.

And the harder Kate pursued that goal, the more vigorous Snow would hunt her.

"You'd sacrifice being a goddess for mortality?"

Snow flicked a few flakes through the air at him and winked. "In the dazzle of a snowflake."

Chapter 7

After a bath, Kate donned a thick white terry robe over a matching black bra and panty set. She liked sexy lingerie. What woman did not? It made her feel great to know beneath her bundle of winter sweaters and long johns and coats and scarves and mittens, the next-to-nothings hugged her skin. Like her body wasn't going completely to waste out here, so far from hot, sexy single men.

It had been her choice to seclude herself. And it wasn't as though she was a hermit. A trip to town once a week found her spending the day, buying groceries, chatting in the café with friends and stopping by the small, but resourceful library. And she never turned down the opportunity to chat with a handsome man.

A lot of strangers visited the town of Ely; it was a tourist hotspot for hunters and outdoor sports enthusiasts headed into the Boundary Waters. This time of year, there were plenty flannel-clad beefy types to choose from, and even a few uber-ripped snowboarders. Sometimes, after a chat, she went out to dinner with the guy. And when in the mood, she even went with the occasional man back to his motel room for sex.

She was a modern woman who didn't need a boyfriend but did enjoy sex. The bonus was the connection and conversation. Most laughed at her profession, or said, "No, really, what do you aspire to do with your life?"

She was aspiring right now, thank you very much. The scientific implications of finding two identical snowflakes could disclose itself to global warming, or who knew what else. She wouldn't know until she found that elusive pair.

Tracing her hand through the air before the window in an arc to match the sweep of frost, she caught a blur of motion out near the window. A bear? The woods were filled with them, though this time of year they should be hibernating. Could be a moose, yet they rarely ventured so close to humans.

"Maybe a raccoon," she said as she opened the door to inspect. And there he sat on the front stoop.

"Should I be worried you've become my stalker?"

"Only if my frequent visits disturb you." Jal turned and beamed a cool gaze up at her. "Do they?"

"No, surprisingly…no. If I'd met you in town—" She would have followed him to his hotel room. "Want to come inside? Or am I right in guessing you like the cold as opposed to the cozy warmth of my home?"

"It's a beautiful evening. The moon is low and full."

Indeed the deep blue night sky was punctuated with a brilliant silver moon and stars too numerous to count.

"Grab a coat and join me, Kate."

"Be right there."

Shuffling her bare feet into the knee-high furry boots lined up by the door, Kate wondered how many levels of disturbing this strange dating scenario qualified for. The few times she'd seen Jal she had been clad in but underwear—as she was again. He seemed to exist in fifteen-degree weather as if it were mere air conditioning. And she was pulling on a jacket over her robe to go sit on an icy cement stoop.

Because the man was hot, and she wanted another kiss from him.

So maybe she was crazy. She'd be sure to leave this little affair of the deranged off her Christmas letter to friends this year.

The thermometer had settled to the teens, and Kate knew she'd last but a few minutes outside without thermal leggings and a cap and mittens. But she counted on some snuggling to prolong the minutes.

"Besides," she muttered, shoving her hands in her pockets, "I'm a born and bred Minnesotan. If I can't take the cold then I should pack up and move."

Heck, it was the one real bragging right Minnesotans had, and Kate was not averse to use it when it suited.

She stepped out and sat, tugging her coat low to sit

on. "The sky is gorgeous," she said. "You don't see stars that bright in a big city. Must be the cold air."

"I like the cold air."

"I guessed that."

"You do, too."

She dipped her gloved hand into the loose snow shoveled high by the step and formed it into a snowball. "Love it, couldn't imagine a world without it." A toss hit the mailbox with a clang. "But I do respect the awesome power of nature and its swift ability to render we mere mortals helpless."

"Yes, a mere mortal." He turned his gaze onto hers. So pale, and seeking, piercing her with an intensity that read her like a scanner, documenting every portion in minute detail. In the darkness Kate was unable to see the dimension of color in his eyes, which was a good thing.

"What are you looking for, Jal?"

"I'm not sure," he said. And he meant it. "I don't believe I've ever looked at eyes the color of yours."

"They're just green."

"They are spring. I don't much like spring."

"I suspect you don't. I could close them." She did so, and leaned into his body to mine some of his warmth. No such luck. The shiny ski jacket held the cold. "Now what do you see?"

"Moonlight on copper." Fingers slid over her hair. "Pure beams of light on pale flesh."

The touch of his ungloved finger made her flinch, but she kept her eyes closed as his fingertip traced the brow of her nose, and under her eyes, and then tickled an icy thrill across her lips.

"What are *you* looking for, Kate?"

She smiled and dipped her head into his palm. "The Norse warrior, I guess."

"I don't understand."

"You don't have to. It's a silly dream."

He nodded, cleared his throat. "Why do you exist, Kate?"

"That's a pretty deep question, Jal."

"I just wonder about things."

"All right then. I exist…" Man, he'd jumped to existential in a flicker. He hadn't struck her as the sort, but she was all for humor especially since she was starting to shiver. "Because I was born."

"Why?"

"Why was I born?" An even quirkier question, but it didn't take much thought. "Because my parents were in love."

"Ah. Love. Tell me about love."

"The long version or the short?"

"Short. You're starting to shiver."

"All right. You want to know why I exist? Love is what it's all about."

"Really? Does love…make you better? More worthy?"

"I don't think so, but it certainly feeds your soul." She snuggled up to him. "Speaking of feeding one's soul, I would like another kiss because I'm starting to really feel the cold."

"My kisses can never make you warm, Kate."

"You are rather chilly. Most guys are warmer than girls. Cold-blooded, probably. But you're wrong about your kisses not making me warm. They light a fire in my veins."

"Impossible."

"You say impossible a lot." She took his hand and held it to the side of her neck. So cold, his flesh, and yet, the sting of it ignited her inner flame. "Are you so unaware your kisses render me hot and bothered? Jal, you undo me."

"With a simple kiss?"

"With a kiss. With your touch. With your presence. I don't know what it is about you, but it's like the frost I find on the window each morning. You speak to me in a language that needs no words."

"But you scraped the frost pattern away. Maybe you'll want to scrape me away if I touch you too much?"

Was the man simple? Perhaps he didn't date a lot of women. It was possible, for his oddness.

"Touch me, Jal, and see how quickly I pull you closer."

"I'd love to touch you all night, Kate. But there are things about me you would never understand."

"Try me."

He hung his head. Considering a confession? "Not tonight. But another kiss in the moonlight, if you please?"

"Yes. No."

Kate stood and tugged the coat tightly across her stomach. She may be open to strange men, but she wasn't desperate, or a glutton for frostbite.

"No more kisses in the freezing air. I like winter, but

not enough to suffer frostbite. If you want to kiss me again, Jal, it's going to have to be inside."

She held the door open for him. Heat from the hearth fire crept over her cheeks on seductive waves. She wanted to melt with the sensation, drip from her clothes, and drown in Jal's kisses.

Jal stood and peered inside her house. What was he afraid of?

"I don't bite," she tried.

He smiled, weakly, and stepped across the threshold, then captured her in an embrace against the door. Fine with her. They were inside. Mostly.

Sensing an oncoming kiss, she pressed her fingers to his cool lips. "Do you live around here?"

"No."

"Then how do you get to my cabin? It's fifteen miles from town. You don't drive. Are you a cross-country skier?"

"Why all the questions? I thought you wanted to kiss."

"A girl's got a right to ask questions of a man standing closer than close, and well, what is it with us that you've seen me in my underwear more than actual clothes?"

"They're very pretty," he said, and tugged open her coat. "Black lace and pink ribbons. You speak of being undone. I don't know what it is you do to me, Kate, but whatever it is, it feels good. Right here." He touched his chest, and then reached for the same spot on Kate's chest. "Can I touch you here, where your flesh curves?"

She caught his hand as he moved in for the play, and

rubbed his fingers vigorously between her palms. "You're cold as ice, buddy. No touching until you warm up."

"I thought you liked my cool kisses?"

"They're awesome." She blew over his fingertips, smiling as he flinched playfully. "But some touches shouldn't be so cold. There. Still cool, but much better."

He snuck a kiss, and smiled against her mouth as his hand moved in for adventure. The cool electricity of his touch, there, between her breasts and tracing the curves, made Kate suck in a breath. She must be thirty degrees warmer than the man.

Delicate coolness trickled over the mound of her breast. Her nipples tightened.

"Hot chocolate," he whispered in her ear. "I smelled it on you that first morning out by the—er, when we first met. You're the sweetest thing, Kate. The sweetest thing I've touched. The sweetest kiss."

He splayed a hand over her breast and massaged her nipple through the black lace.

"So I'm a sweet girl. You know, that's not necessarily a compliment."

"It isn't?" He leaned down to kiss where his fingers pinched her nipple.

"Oh, that's good, that's…"

"Sweet?"

"I don't want to be sweet, Jal. I want to be—"

"So hot."

"Yes."

"Sticky with need." The shivery trail of his touch glided across her bare stomach, circling her belly button.

Though he was noticeably cool, fire blazed in the wake of his explorations. And when he tugged her lace panties over a hip and slid his hand behind the lace, Kate tossed back her head and moaned appreciatively.

"You like this?" he murmured against the lace of her bra. Two of his fingers found a rhythm and massaged her aching, moist sex. "Here is where you truly are fire. It's the only fire I can ever be near. You burn me, Kate."

His rhythm increased, and while he dizzied her senses with an exquisite mastery, he scattered nipping kisses from breast to breast. Felt like sharp snow crystals pinging her skin. Very sexy. Uniquely Jal.

Kate clung to the back of the sofa. The heavy parka slid from her shoulders down to her wrists. Jal's ski coat slithered against her thighs. She wanted to arch farther back, opening herself completely to him, but when climax verged, she snapped forward, wrapping herself about Jal, squeezing her thighs around his hand and crying out against his neck.

If two bodies could mist, theirs did. Kate's heat simmered across Jal's cool flesh. Tendrils of steam coiled about their half-clad embrace. Jal kissed the crown of Kate's head and held her until the final shudders of her gorgeous climax slipped away.

Frost faeries never came like this. They usually shuddered to bits, literally, at climax. A dissatisfying end to his quest to slake lust.

He licked Kate's fire from his finger. Delicious, but so hot. Too hot for him?

Unsure, he looked to the door. Not completely closed, a wave of cool air hissed across the side of his face. His flesh, this human flesh he wore appeared vividly bright, growing deeper in color, blazing like fire.

Kate could not know how dangerous it was to touch her. Yet he was torn between racing for the door and dipping his head down to suck one of her nipples into his mouth.

When she tugged insistently at the fly of his ski pants, he quickly decided.

"Until we meet again," he whispered and tipped up Kate's chin to kiss her on the mouth.

"No, you can't leave. Stay, Jal, we've only just—"

Another kiss stole away the plead he couldn't bear to hear. This is how it had to be. He didn't do things like this with humans. It destroyed his focus.

Could she melt him? Was that why his chest ached so fiercely?

"I've business," he summoned the lie. "A flight to catch."

"No."

Even as he unwrapped her legs from around his hips, she kissed him, teasing him back into the flame. Hell, he wanted to find his satisfaction. Was there happiness in making love to Kate? He craved it. But he couldn't know how long before being inside this toasty home would harm him.

"I'll return when I can."

And he kissed her wanting mouth, quickly, wistfully, and then turned and walked out.

He cleared the drive and entered the forest before plunging himself into the snow and reviving his natural state. It took longer than usual for the human costume to release its heat and begin to crystallize into rugged hoarfrost before finally particulating into fine crystals.

"She will undo me," he thought, as he took to the air.

Chapter 8

He'd done what he must to get himself out from Kate's death embrace. Yes, her warm, wanting body could prove deadly. Maybe. Well, he wasn't exactly sure.

So after Jal finished a minor job on the peak of the Alps—taking out a Fortune 500 boss who was single-handedly responsible for clearing thousands of acres of rainforest—he headed home to Nordika to find Ice.

His cousin Ice was an easy-going fellow who had taken Jal under wing, so to speak, when he'd first been deemed Frost, and had shown him the ways of their kind. Ice was always wrapped within the arms or legs of a sexy ice faery. If Ice wasn't freezing the entire northern hemisphere, then he was having sex. Something about a constant ice-hard-on...

Frost was relieved to find his cousin kissing a giggling ice faery *goodbye* as he arrived at his estate. A swanky palace completely of ice, accented with hematite columns polished to a chrome gleam. The ice god lived the high life.

"Frost, my man." Ice, still in the human-shaped ice form he assumed to have sex with one of his folk, offered an open-armed gesture.

Jal reformed his crystals into human form and leaned in for a brief hug from Ice. He didn't touch the god long; his frost hardened and began to crack. There was a reason neither of them had ever considered shagging Snow. Neither wanted to risk rearranging their crystal structure.

"She was gorgeous," Jal commented on the slender faery who likely dispersed into thousands of diminutive ice folk the moment she'd left the palace.

"I never do anything less than gorgeous, man. So what's up with you? I saw your work on the Brooklyn Bridge last week. Cars sliding this way and that while photographers scrambled to take pictures. Splendid!"

"Thanks. I was pleased with that creation myself. But you! That lobster boat in the Atlantic the other day?"

"Froze it in place right in the middle of the ocean. Sweet, eh?"

"Nice." Jal strode along the wall formed by a crisscross of laser-precision ice bars. "You are the master, Ice."

"You know it. No one ever poked an eye out with a frost pattern. You need an icicle for that."

"I concede to greatness," Frost said and offered a mock bow. He snapped a finger against an ice beam and it rang as if fine crystal. "So, Ice…you talk to Snow lately?"

"Are you kidding? That female is just nasty lately. I think it's that time of the century, you know? Crabby and belligerent, and all in your face about any little thing. No, I've kept my distance."

That time of the century? Jal smirked. "She's influenced Old Man Winter. Actually got him to somehow order me on a superfluous hunt."

"The chick who's looking for two identical snowflakes?"

"You know about her?"

Ice grinned a clear smile. "She used to skate on me when she was younger. Nice legs on that Wilson girl."

"Yes, they are rather fine."

And when wrapped about his hips, all the finer. Jal touched the icy sail of a decorative crystal ship, imbuing his frost across the frozen water. Recalling Kate in his arms made his thoughts so warm, he wasn't sure if he'd start melting right here. "She is exquisite."

"Frost, I know that tone."

"What tone?"

Ice's frozen grin grew even wider and he winked. "You're lusting after a human woman. Those snowflakes in your eyes are the closest things to stars we'll ever have."

"Nonsense. I am detached and uncaring."

"You want her, I know it."

Frost sighed out crystals. "So what if I do?"

"Long as you don't get too close, is all I'm saying."

"Too close? Ice, I've kissed her."

"Nice." The god rubbed his chin with ice fingers.

"What did she think about that? You being colder than outer space and all?"

"She didn't mind it. Ice, it felt like fire to kiss her."

"That is not good."

"Not real fire. In here." He clapped a palm over his chest. Frost crystals scattered to the ice rink floor. "Right here…it…it aches. Whenever I'm around her. And even when I'm not. I feel like I…want something. Like right now? I can only think about returning to the warm cabin and kissing her again and touching her, and—but I can't."

"Why not, man? Sounds like fine recreation from the death and karmic-repayment bit to me."

"We Winter gods can't touch human flesh for long, can we? I've never been attracted to a human before. This is the first time I've touched one and have not given them frostbite."

"Because you were in human flesh form."

"Yes, but Kate's warmth… Won't it destroy me?"

"Ah, you're worried about a major meltdown. Won't happen, man. Trust me. She might send your mercury popping through the glass, but you don't need to worry about melting if you have sex with her. Trust me. So long as you cool down as quickly as possible after the fun, you'll be fine."

"Sounds like you've experience with this."

"Maybe. See, man, touching the woman's flesh can melt you. Slowly. Not so quickly you can't do it with her for a good while before you start to feel sort of…squishy." Ice averted his gaze south on Jal's anatomy, and then quickly glanced away. "You'll know what I'm talking about when that happens. Anyway, if she can take your chill, I'd say go for it."

"I won't give her frostbite in any uncomfortable places?"

"Not unless you want to."

He could induce frostbite when in frost form, which wasn't going to happen around Kate. Never. Besides, he'd touched her intimately without causing anything more than orgasm. What a spectacular success that had been.

Ice snapped his fingers smartly, focusing Frost's attention. "It's not the warmth of a human we Winter gods need fear, but emotion."

Jal mouthed the word, "Emotion." He nodded, though he wasn't entirely sure what Ice meant.

"It's a killer," Ice said. "When you start feeling and pining for the woman. Like that ache you're talking about? It's your heart, man. Trust me, we gods do have hearts, and we can love and hate with the best of them."

"I thought we only lusted?"

"That's what you've been led to believe. If you don't know love than you need never fear it, right?"

"Snow mentioned love. I'm not sure what it is. But if it's this ache inside, then I don't want it to stop."

"Razor ice," Ice swore. "You're already falling for her."

Frost clapped a hand over his chest. "Falling?"

"In love, Frost. Love. To whisper *I love you* to the woman—and mean it—could be your death. She's not like you and I."

"I know that. She is flesh, and I am not."

"Exactly. We were meant for Nordika, she for the mortal realm. If you lose your heart to her, then it's as if you've ripped it out and left it to melt on her doorstep *in springtime*. That part of you doesn't belong in the mortal realm. It *can't* belong there."

"So I can never have love?" What had she said? *Love feeds your soul.*

"Hell yes, you can. Hook up with one of your frost folk. Not that I'd recommend falling in love with one of those silly bits, but you know."

No, he wasn't interested in the vapid, unfocused frost folk whom he conjured to serve him both out in the mortal world, and here in Nordika on a more intimate level. They never lasted longer than a day or so.

"So I can give Kate physical pleasure, but I can never give her my heart?"

"Exactly."

"Shouldn't be too difficult. I have sex with my folk all the time. They come. They leave. I never think about them again. I can do this." No problem. Love would be experienced, and then onward to the next challenge. "Thanks, Ice. It was good talking to you."

"Yeah, man, no problem. Hope to see you again."

Jal walked out of the palace, yet didn't hear Ice's last words. "Think that one's a goner, he is. Wonder how soon it'll take to find a replacement for Frost?"

A bowl of chicken noodle soup sat cooling near the computer monitor. Kate's throat was scratchy, as if she had a cold, yet she felt great. No body aches or sniffles.

She hadn't any cherry lozenges to suck on, so soup would have to serve.

She had catalogued yesterday's photos. Now she sat staring at the image of the frost pattern she'd snapped days earlier.

"Sorry? It really is there in the frost. A word. But why *sorry?* Who would want to apologize to me? Did Jal trace the word into the glass?"

Frost could be manipulated to form designs on windows and metal surfaces by introducing scratches or even finger smears. She had tried a few times and had created geometric designs. It had made for a cool eighth grade science project. There were actually frost artists who snapped photos of their creations. No different than her snowflake photographs, but they did manipulate nature, while she did not.

This morning her window had been clear and frost free. A bit of a letdown. Was it so weird to want to see more frost on her window? Like a message from a lover, she took giddy joy in seeing the intricate patterns.

A sip of noodles and chicken broth ended lunch. "Yuck. Cold."

Kate set the bowl in the sink, and then poured herself a glass of red wine. It warmed in her mouth and didn't so much sooth her sore throat as make her care less if it did hurt. The sky was overcast today. For some reason she didn't feel like getting all bundled up and hauling her equipment out to snap pictures. If she were getting a cold, a day of rest sounded perfect.

Her camera had not been damaged in the freak avalanche, thanks to the hard case exterior. The tripod and the staging platform she used to collect snowflakes were a little twisted, but with a wrench and some muscle, she figured they could be fixed.

Sucking in the corner of her lip, images of Jal formed in her brain. The touch of him as he'd glided his hands over her body last night. Jal had not only made her climax, he'd pressed her *on* button, and she hadn't come down since.

Gliding her hand between her legs, she squeezed her thighs together, and the tingling scurried throughout her loins. A delicious reminder of his mastery.

"That man really knows how to touch a woman." She sipped the wine. "But how to keep him around for longer than it takes me to orgasm? Not that there's anything wrong with a quickie. What is with that guy?"

Mysterious didn't even come close to describing Jal. Enigmatic. Sexy. Elusive.

If she were smart, she'd bolt her doors and not allow him entrance until she saw a legitimate ID, a work badge and probably a car or practical means of travel. Yet, opening the door to Jal was a thoughtless, automatic act. She couldn't deny him.

Because he was different from any other person. Physically, she thought there were moments when his flesh appeared of ice, vivid with color and luminous. She knew it was impossible. People were not like nature. Perhaps the man had a connection to nature she could not imagine?

"Disturbing," she muttered. "He's not even here, and I can't concentrate enough to work."

She turned on the water to rinse her dishes, and then spied a movement outside her front window. "Oh!"

Kate hurried to the window. Tight, spiraling coils and long feathery plumes formed what looked like… "A bouquet of flowers?"

And then a face appeared in the window, and her heart leapt. "Jal?" She rushed to open the door. "It's you! You scared me."

"Was it a good, heart-racing scare?" Cool fingers slipped inside her terry robe and—she hadn't dressed since her shower—the shock of his icy touch lasted so long as it took her to meld against his body and kiss him.

"You brought me flowers?" she asked.

"You like them?"

"Frost flowers. They're gorgeous. Your job finished?"

"Huh? Oh, yes. Had a…er, good flight back. I'm free for the day, actually. And some hot chocolate."

"I could put some on the stove?"

"Actually, I like the hot chocolate running in your veins, Kate. My sweet, sweet Kate. I want you, Kate."

"Oh, yes, that sounds—yes."

He slipped the robe from her shoulders and it fell to the floor. As quickly, he shrugged off his silver suit coat. Beneath he wore a shimmery white shirt, run through with silver threading. The silky fabric glided over Kate's bare flesh as he teased her ruched nipples.

"The door isn't completely closed," Kate muttered, but it didn't matter. Be damned the high heating bills. Who could care when the sultan of cool had just stripped her in one masterful move?

"Mmm, touch me, Jal. Set me on fire."

He walked her up the step and toward her bed. Kneeling on the patchwork quilt, Kate pulled him to her and unbuttoned his shirt. His flesh was pale, but hard as the ice coloring his eyes.

The thick vein on the underside of his elbow bulged. She traced a finger along it, sliding higher to the muscle on his bicep. He sucked in a breath and unbuttoned his pants. The sound of his restrained desire spurred her on. Licking over his shoulder, she reached his neck, where a sexy vampire nip stirred a satisfying moan from her lover.

"You tease me, Kate."

A shimmy of her hips rubbed her nipples across his chest. "What are you going to do about it?"

The arc of his brow spoke of devious mischief. And his tickling touch along her waist reduced Kate to a delicious shiver. He didn't relent, and quickly found the most ticklish spot on her body. Lifting one of her bare feet, he lashed his tongue across the arch.

"Oh, no," she pleaded. "I'm such a spaz when I'm tickled. I don't want to kick you."

He gripped her foot firmly. A glitter of naughtiness twinkled in his eyes. He licked the underside of her biggest toe. Kate cringed and laughed at the same time.

He struggled to hold her foot but would not cease his torment. Such unabashed playfulness felt a reward after weeks of self-imposed exile. And though she could no longer catch her breath to laugh, Kate gasped and winced as each slow lash of his wintry tongue shivered waves of melting laughter through her bones.

And then she clutched the edge of the bed, gripping the patchwork quilt. The tickle had changed to pleasure and the slow trace of his tongue guided an erotic tingle into her groin. And swirling higher across her abdomen and at her breasts.

"Oh, my God, I can't believe this," she managed. "All these years I've been so ticklish. But if I'd known—oh, Jal, that's so good."

"I'm just getting started." And though her toes waggled at the loss of his attention, the next hot spot started humming as he kissed the rise of her anklebone.

Jal moved slowly, attending to every inch of her body. As if he were learning her, marking her every curve, rise and indent, his mouth took her measure. To the back of her calves, and around to glide his fingers aside her knees. A dash of tongue there at the back of her knee titillated. Kate tucked her head into the goose-down pillow and bit the corner of it.

At once Kate felt as if she were involved in an illicit liaison that would prompt an admonishing finger wave from voyeurs—and then she didn't care. This was her pleasure. To own. Be damned, the vibrator. When had she abandoned real men?

Jal's rigid nipples skimmed her thighs as he bent to kiss her mons. He tickled her there with his tongue, nestling deep within her sex, but much as she desired it, he didn't give a repeat performance of last night. Instead, he continued his journey up, over the small rise on her tummy and along the angles of her ribcage.

Kate clung to the mattress as if it were a ship floating

in the ocean. Each wave threatened to suck her down into sweet oblivion. She wanted to drown, to know if Jal's strong arms would catch her. But not too quickly. She preferred a lingering, slow death.

A lash to her nipple strummed a giddy cord that stretched from breasts to between her legs, and Kate cried out. The silky weave of his pants stroked her thighs.

"Your pants," she said tightly. "Off. Quickly."

"As my lady commands." The zip and toss happened in a blur. Jal lay upon her and kissed her mouth. Roughly. Wickedly. He bruised her with his urgency. "My fire, Kate, my death."

"Don't stop. We can drown together."

She reached down and encircled his cock. Heavy and hard like a column of marble. Directing him inside her, she shivered at his bold entrance. The uniqueness of him fascinated her—and rocketed her desire through the roof.

He moved but a few times inside her, sliding his hardness masterfully, claiming her with each thrust. And then she let go, sinking, drowning and loving him for the fatality.

Chapter 9

Jal startled out of sleep and blew strands of copper hair from his face. Cold fire, the silken strands. Everything about Kate Wilson blazed across his being and left him marked, as if scarred by flame.

When he'd plunged inside her body the burn of her had enveloped him in a wondrous lost dream. He'd never imagined heat could feel so incredible. So freeing. So connective. He'd felt a part of Kate. It was not a feeling he'd ever known before.

Love? Truly. It was an amazing feeling.

He'd touched a human and had not melted.

What Snow had said to him returned. *A chosen changeling is born in the mortal realm.*

He'd been born to mortals? That meant he had once

been human, like Kate. They had more in common than he'd first thought.

Did that mean he could have love? Ice had fiercely warned against it. Do the deed, but don't let the heart begin to feel.

No, he must not. Jal pushed the warm ache aside. The world needed him. He mustn't allow one gorgeous woman to distract him beyond this brief interlude into pleasure. It had been a foray into happiness, not love. And he must be satisfied with that.

He rolled onto his side. Kate slumbered beside him. Moonlight shivered across her flat belly. He reached to touch her but pulled back. Angling his head level with her stomach he eyed the faint steam brewing up from her flesh. Probably human eyes could not see it.

Though there was no fire in the hearth, the blankets and sheets and—hell, the afterglow of sex, made him feel heavy and a little disoriented.

"Have to cool off. Now."

Grabbing his clothes, because to leave them behind would cause Kate more questions, he slid off the bed. But he didn't bother to dress. Dashing across the wood floor, he paused in the open doorway and turned an eye to the bed. She didn't rouse.

He hated to leave her looking so luscious, smelling so delicious. And oh, her sweet moans as his every touch had imprinted her shape, texture and fire upon him.

"I'll be back," he whispered, and stepped outside into the below zero air.

* * *

It was not disconcerting to wake and find Jal's side of the bed empty. Kate shrugged it off as another of his eccentricities. Besides, her morning perkiness might scare the man. Best he learned that side of her gradually.

She tripped off to the shower, humming a Christmas tune. She giggled to think of her Jack Frost, her cool but sensuous lover, nipping at her toes last night.

"Oh, yeah!" Her enthusiasm echoed in the shower, and she didn't emerge until the entire room was drenched in steam.

Shrugging into undies and yoga pants, she forewent a bra in favor of a neat fur-lined sweater she'd picked up last month after a shopping trip to Minneapolis. The feel of the luxurious, albeit fake, fur against her nipples should be illegal.

"So freakin' good," she muttered as she went to mix up some hot chocolate. "But not nearly so nice as Jal licking my nipples."

A surprise coughing attack bent her over the countertop. She hadn't noticed in the steamy shower, but now, the scratch had returned to her throat. It ached and felt as if sharp ice cubes bumped down her esophagus.

"But I don't feel sick," she muttered. "I hope I'm not coming down with something. I'd hate to give it to Jal."

The microwave dinged. Sipping the cinnamon-laced hot chocolate soothed her throat. Absently, she slid her hand across her sweater. The fur caressed her hard nipple. It was going to be a long day without him around.

Distraction was in order. She'd work on her equipment and check the weather report for snow. Fingers crossed, snow would fall, and she'd have work to do.

Kate strolled to the computer desk—but halfway there, choked on the hot liquid. "Holy…"

The front window glittered with sunlight—and another frost pattern. This one said *Sweet*.

Kate blinked. But she didn't struggle with the bizarre impossibility of the situation. She knew there were no intelligent spiders braving the chill to leave her love notes. No, a sexy frost artist had left behind another of his masterpieces.

"Sweet? Yeah, well you are crazy sexy cool, Mr. Frosti. Heh." She sat down before the computer.

"Frosti. I've my own Jack Frost for the holidays. He's even cool enough to qualify. Bet he could wear snowflakes on his lips and they'd not melt."

Yet, he could melt *her* with but a dash of his masterful tongue.

"Oh, baby." And she shivered one of those good after-sex shivers that tingled in her loins and breasts. A cough quickly chased away the feeling.

Kate stroked her throat. "Have I been kissing too much? Am I getting mono?" Jal's kisses, while amazing, had been met with his wintergreen cool breath. "Maybe I'm allergic to his kisses? Nah."

Clasping the mug of hot chocolate and drawing up a knee to her chest, she checked the printer. No printout waited, which was odd, but only until she recalled she had taken yesterday off. No data to review today.

She had to fix her equipment. She wasn't going to

become a millionaire sipping hot drinks and dreaming about sex with Jack Frost.

"I'll go out and snap more pictures this afternoon. After a nice toasty fire and some oatmeal for breakfast."

Decided, she set to retrieving a couple logs from outside and around back of the cabin. After breakfast, she filled a tin bucket with water, which she always kept by the door in case of emergencies—she had a fire extinguisher, too, but one can never be too prepared— she then settled before the crackling fire with her crumpled equipment to assess the damage.

The tripod was easily bent back into shape. The staging table where she caught snowflakes was a loss, but by replacing it with black foam, she could get some photos taken today after all.

There was a knock at her door. Jal poked his head in and called her name. "Did you miss me, Kate?"

"I did!" She looked up from the floor where she sat amongst scattered parts and gestured him over. "Come sit by the fire with me."

"Uh, that's fine. Maybe I'll just…" He eyed the bucket of water near the door. "You plan on creating an ice rink today?"

"No, it's in case of fire."

"Right. Fire. You are the queen of fire."

"You don't want to snuggle with me?" She pouted appropriately. "I missed you."

"Come over here—" he waggled a finger sugges- tively "—and I'll make you forget I was ever gone."

"Sounds promising." She joined him by the door. A

hug fit her body against his hard muscled form. "Are you allergic to heat or something? You don't like to get too hot, do you?"

"It's fire. I…have a thing about it."

"Childhood scare?"

"Something like that."

"Poor guy. We can snuggle on the couch before the window where it's kinda cool."

Kate muffled a cough behind a fist and Jal gently smoothed his fingers over her throat. "What's the cough from?"

"Not sure. I'm not sick. I've been spending too much time in below-zero weather. Though that makes little sense. Weather does not make a person sick. My throat is just scratchy. Maybe I've been kissing you too much."

His reaction wasn't at all teasing, instead Jal's eyes widened, then he quickly looked away. "So what are you up to over there?"

"Assessing the damage to my equipment. The camera survived. I'm heading out for more pictures this afternoon."

"How long before you think you'll find matching snowflakes? Those elusive doubles?"

"Maybe tomorrow. Maybe never. It's a long shot."

"Then why even attempt it? Is it the money?"

"Money is nice but it doesn't buy happiness. I do it because the process is very rewarding."

"How so?"

"Well, I've published a book of my pictures, with another slated for publication next winter, which allows me to live this sheltered lifestyle of the cold and slightly eccentric. I'm pretty much the only snowflakologist in the country, so my advice and knowledge is sought, on occasion, which I enjoy. But you know…"

"What?"

"I just want people to believe. To see nature as I do. No one has ever believed in what I see."

"I do."

"Yes, I think you do. Too bad the rest of the world isn't like you. But Jal, I mean it when I say I see nature as it is. It's three dimensional and breathes with all the colors of the rainbow. A simple rock isn't solid and plain to me. It has depth. Insides. A soul."

"Of course it does. Humans don't usually see nature that way?"

"Humans? Jal, you're the strangest guy sometimes. No, humans only see the outside of things. And you, I see you, Jal. You're a part of nature, aren't you?"

His jaw muscle tensed. He took the fingers she stroked along his cheek and kissed them. "I am." He looked aside and down.

"What's wrong? You don't seem yourself today. You're not having regrets about last night?"

"Regret making love with you? Never." His kiss renewed the giddy tingles of last night's encounter.

Jal had but to touch her stomach and glide his finger across her flesh. The stir of orgasm snuck upon her.

"Lower," she whispered into his kiss. "Make me yours, Jal. You know exactly how to touch me, to make me come."

"I like playing with your fire. You are like no other

woman." His fingers slid between her legs, finding the easy rhythm he'd mastered last night. "You make me feel things I've never experienced before."

"Really? I can't imagine what."

"Things like companionship, playfulness, a desire born of true want and not a simple reflex. Happiness."

"All that from one night of lovemaking? You don't date often, do you, Jal?"

"I don't date at all— Wh-what's that sound?"

Kate listened. Even while orgasm charged upon her, she was able to focus outside her body's surrender to Jal—and she felt the strange disturbance. Something wasn't right. Clinging to Jal's shoulders, she opened her eyes. The front window darkened and an immense thud literally shook her home. The windowpane cracked and glass shattered inside.

Jal lifted Kate from the couch and pushed her back toward the hearth. Overhead, the ceiling beams creaked. Wood dust sifted down in buff-colored clouds.

"What is that?" she shouted. "Feels like a train hit my house."

"I'm not sure. This is not normal?"

"Normal? There's snow packed up against the house and it blew out my front window. No, that's not a normal snow storm."

"Snow— She did not!"

Jal rushed to the door and flung it open. A litter of snowflakes sifted inside, tumbling to loose heaps at his feet. It had banked halfway up the doorway opening. He scrambled up the packed wall of white.

"Jal! Stay inside! If it was an avalanche—"

Kate stopped herself before she ran barefoot through the shattered glass. "Avalanche? What am I saying? I live on flat land with gentle slopes surrounded by tall pine trees. An avalanche is impossible in Minnesota."

So what had happened? Snowstorms didn't drop what looked like four feet of snow in seconds. And she didn't live at the bottom of a hill or mountain.

This is insane. What is he doing?

Stuffing her feet into her boots, Kate then scrambled for her gloves.

She heard shouts outside. Jal's voice. And…a woman?

"You will not do this, Snow!"

Jal tromped across the thick, wet snow, his fleshed-out human-formed feet sinking deeply. The heaviest, deadliest snow was dense with water and would suffocate a mortal if buried in the stuff.

Taking frost form, Jal retained human shape.

Snow stood at the top of her disaster, brilliant in her cold beauty. She thrust out a hand and sent a blast of ice crystals at Jal. They were large and deadly, razor-edged ninja snowstars.

One menacing flake pierced Jal's forehead and cut through. Snapping out a curse, he shook off the pain. Ichor dripped onto his nose. He quickly reformed.

"I didn't know you'd be here, Frost. What's up with you and the bitch?"

"She is not— I won't allow you to harm Kate. She

had nothing to do with not getting chosen as your replacement. Killing her isn't going to change things."

"It's worth a shot." Snow blew again. This time Jal ducked. A focused blizzard soared over his head. "Come on, Frost. Show me what you're made of."

"Indeed?" Spinning about, he unleashed a fury of sharp hoar frost that cut through Snow's form and embedded deep in her flakes. "You like that?"

"Ouch." Snow shook off his frost, but the hoar clung tenaciously to her flakes.

"How do you do it? Get Winter to do your bidding?"

"I asked nicely."

With a stomp of her foot, Snow set the thick layer of snow beneath Jal's feet to an unsteady wobble. The liquid evaporated and the flakes hardened. He fell through the fine, powdered depths up to his waist.

Feeling the water level increase, Jal quickly transformed to a crystal fog and soared toward Snow, who beat at him with her snow crystal fists, but missed each time.

He landed behind her, assuming human shape, and breathed a command to his folk. The air crackled with legions of frost folk. They chattered and skimmed the frozen air, glinting in the anemic winter sunlight.

With a gesture, Jal sent them toward Snow, but she summoned her own army, and the air hissed with the clash of frost and snow.

What Kate saw on her front yard should have made her scream. Instead, she lost grip on the ice-hard packed snow, slipped down the embankment before her door, and slid into her living room.

"What the hell? He's— And he's battling a—"

She couldn't vocalize what she'd witnessed. It was something that only happened in movies enhanced by expensive CGI effects.

Not real beings. Maybe? Snowflakes and hoarfrost, and they seemed to…battle?

Gripping the edge of the tin water bucket, Kate's scattered thoughts cohered to form a conclusion. Not necessarily a rational one, but a working plan. She had to stop whatever was happening out front. And the only way to settle a snow and frost storm?

Lugging up the water bucket, she fit her boots into the packed snow, taking steps to the surface that leveled with her rooftop. The air was white with snowflakes. But they moved purposefully, not fluttering to ground, as they should. Back and forth and up and down and frenzied.

And the creature composed of frost pummeled the strange feminine-shaped snowman.

"Snowperson," Kate corrected her thoughts. "I'm going to need some serious therapy after this."

Kate swung up the bucket and doused the battle with water.

Flakes melted, some froze, others dispersed to powder, but all ceased whatever it was they were doing.

Eaten in half by the water, the snow creature quickly dissipated. Though Kate couldn't be sure the whiff of snow stirred up by the wind wasn't part of the same creature.

And the frost man—thing, *person?*—froze, one arm lunged out to swing a punch. As quickly, the ice cracked and hoarfrost jutted out from the human-shaped figure, growing at an impossible pace. A figure that wore Jal's face.

"Oh, my God." Stumbling backward, Kate's boot slipped from the snow. She scrambled as she fell, dragging huge clods of snow down with her and into the foyer.

"Kate, no!"

The thing shouted at her. In Jal's voice.

Not a thing. It was…her lover?

She grabbed the door and tried to shove it closed. Kicking at the packed clods of snow, she scraped her boot along the floor to clear it from the threshold.

The frost man appeared above at the rim of the snow bank. "Kate, please."

"No!" She slammed the door and struggled with the chain lock. Her fingers shook horribly, and her breath misted from the cold.

A glance to the side spied the broken window. Packed snow completely blocked entrance to the cabin. She was safe, unless he tried to dig through.

A thudding beat upon the door sent a wicked vibration through her heart.

"Kate? Please open the door."

She shook her head, unable to voice her fear.

That's what happens when you invite strangers into your house. They become frost monsters.

Kate shook her head, but no amount of thrashing would erase what she had just witnessed.

"Let me touch you. Then you will see me as I have been. Kate?"

Stepping away from the door, she stared at the unvarnished wood as if to look hard enough would summon an image of Jal to the fore.

But what image? The handsome Norse warrior her latent snow queen had only dreamed would sweep her away? Or the awful image of a frost creature made entirely of...

Frost?

The pounding at the door stopped. Kate sank to her knees and began to cry.

Chapter 10

Kate sat on the snow-wet living room floor for over an hour. When a chunk of compressed snow fell through the broken window, she sniffed back tears and shook herself out of her stunned state.

"Right. Major disaster in my living room. Must do something about it or I'll freeze to death tonight."

It took her three tries to correctly dial the number for the carpenter in town, she still shook so much. Roger Barnes was one of those hire-a-husband handymen. He said he'd be to Kate's cabin in less than an hour, and not to worry.

"Yeah, right," Kate said as she hung up. "But how to explain the avalanche in my front yard when he gets here?"

A flash of the strange battle she'd witnessed notched up her shivers.

The compulsion to step outside and survey the havoc in the front yard pushed her to crawl up the snow pack before the stoop. The yard was four feet higher than ground level, due to the heavily packed snow.

Her breath hushed out in a cloud as she crept on all fours across the top of the snow. The snow glinted and pulsed and glowed with depth.

"Not a single footprint," she noticed.

Nor was there a depression where the water she'd thrown at the battle should have settled into the snow. Everywhere, ice crystals glittered in the sunlight. Big crystals.

"Like hoarfrost, but…not."

Kate bent low to inspect a thin formation of snow and frost and ice. "I need a closer look."

Retrieving a handheld magnifier she kept in her coat pocket, Kate gasped when the low-magnification revealed very strange snow crystals. The formations were about a quarter of an inch, which was large for a snowflake.

"Almost looks like—no, can't be." She studied one formation, then another. "Little arms and legs and—People?"

Impossible.

"Nothing is impossible," she muttered. "The camera will show me the truth."

An hour later, Kate had taken dozens of shots of the crystal formations on her front yard. Roger, the carpenter, had called to say he'd had to replace a snow chain on his truck, so give him another hour.

Meanwhile, she loaded the digital pictures onto the computer. While she waited for iPhoto to sort them, she surfed online and Googled *snow battle,* which didn't pan out. *Frost fights* brought up nothing, save a reference to Alan Frost, a lightweight boxer.

The notion to type in *Jack Frost* brought up a few sites that explained the mythological creature.

"Norse myth names him Jakul Frosti?" She tapped her fingers on her lip and tried to remember the original name Jal had given her. "Vij—something or other."

It hadn't been Jakul. But the last name had definitely been Frosti.

Could he be?

"Nah," she muttered. That was myth. Folklore. A creature made of frost? A physical and scientific impossibility. "Thought you believed in the impossible, Kate, you insane woman."

A stream of coughs bent her double. "I still don't feel sick. Is this what happens when you kiss—" No, she wouldn't say it.

Not without proof.

All the sites summarized various versions of Jack Frost. He was either a god or a faery, or both, according to which nation's legend a person chose to believe. Jack Frost was usually benevolent, creating delicate frost pictures and nipping at caroler's noses around Christmas time—but not always.

Jack Frost, the god, was attributed to assassinating

those mortals who caused irrevocable harm to the environment.

"Sort of a hitman for trees, eh?"

Kate dropped her head and shook it. "No, that's just weird."

And yet, he had been very interested in how her work impacted the environment.

Pushing back in her chair, she couldn't remove the image of Jal, in a weird frost form, battling that snow monster. She had seen it with her own eyes. She was not delusional; only slightly eccentric.

"He does like the cold. And he never seems to completely warm up. Oh, God, he can't be. Can he?"

She tapped the mouse over a woodcut of a dancing faery with knees kicking high as it created frost patterns on the window. Another click opened up the pictures she'd taken from the front yard.

The images showed at three hundred percent, filling her twenty-four inch monitor, and clearly revealing what they were.

"No way."

Kate clicked on the next photo. And the next. The outline of the form. The tiny features. The…wings?

"Little snow people?"

But none had moved, which meant they must be…

"I've a front yard filled with dead frost creatures? They have wings." She traced the tiny wings on one of the forms. "And faces, and limbs and…is this what Jal is, too?"

Realizing the truth with a gulp, Kate pushed back in the chair. When the computer screen seemed to shout at her with clear evidence of something so unreal, she moved the mouse to the corner to bring up a screen saver of falling snowflakes.

"Kate, you seriously screwed up, woman. I do believe you've been having sex with the real Jack Frost."

Roger arrived ten minutes after her startling revelation and helped Kate sweep up the glass and shovel away the snow from the front of the cabin. He reported the framework was still intact, and marveled at the weird avalanche that couldn't be possible had he not seen all the snow himself.

Kate boiled some pasta and heated up a jar of Alfredo sauce while Roger pounded away, extra nails jutting from the corner of his mouth. She fed him and sent him off with a check for his services, and when he offered to look back on her tomorrow, she accepted.

Because even if she had nothing to fear from her strange otherworldly lover, there was still the mystery regarding the snow plowing into the cabin and that other snow creature. And the winged snow people.

Was that it? They'd engaged in a literal battle outside her home? Over what? And why was Jal involved?

Did she seriously believe she'd had sex with Jack Frost?

"I can go there."

Much easier, she felt sure, than the average woman who had never dreamed of being a snow queen as a child.

"You're going to accept him, just like that?" she wondered as she washed the dishes and set them aside on a dishtowel to dry. "He's made of freaking frost, for heaven's sake. How can he— How did he—"

Touch her without melting. Kiss her. Put himself inside her and master her as no other man had.

He could do all that if he were a solid, human man. He had felt like a normal man. All his parts had worked the way they should. And those lips really could serve some amazing kisses.

Did gods have special powers to change to human form?

Kate smirked. "I'm dating a god," she singsonged, but couldn't find the appropriate enthusiasm. What *was* the appropriate enthusiasm?

Or was he like those tiny crystal people she'd snapped pictures of? Did Jal have wings? "I'm sleeping with a faery?"

That didn't sound as exciting, or virile, as a god.

Dropping the wet dishrag in the sink and leaning over the dishes to stretch out her arms and close her eyes, Kate sniffed back a surprise tear.

"I find the coolest guy ever, and he turns out to be literally cool. So cool he's frost."

Isn't this what she'd always dreamed of?

"My dream was *I* was the snow queen."

What about the Norse warrior?

"Yes, but I never imagined he'd be—oh, Kate, what are you doing? You can accept this. Maybe. Unless he never comes back. I dumped water on him. I could have turned him to ice. Not that he isn't already sort of ice. Frost is basically ice crystals, as is snow—oh, Kate, who cares! He's Jack Frost!"

* * *

He inspected the wood planks hammered over the front of Kate's missing window. Good work. He was glad she'd found someone to do this for her.

Himself, he might have created a window of frost for her, but it wouldn't have kept her nearly so warm as real building materials.

Behind him, the snow the Snow goddess had dropped down in an angry fit had melted by half. Miniscule bodies of snow and frost folk lay scattered across the surface. They had given all for the fight.

A nod of acknowledgement for the fallen, and then he stepped up the stoop and lifted his hand. Dare he knock?

Kate had seen him in his natural state. A human wasn't supposed to see such things. And Jal was seriously worried word would get back to Old Man Winter, and he'd be out of a job. Snow couldn't tell without revealing she'd been seen, too. But if she was so miserable as Snow goddess, then perhaps the secret would be worth spilling?

Jal couldn't stay away from this cabin. Not when he didn't know what Snow's next move might be. The goddess had it in for Kate, and gave no sign of ceasing her angry vengeance.

What was so wrong with waiting it out another thousand years for the next Snow to be born? A god could track years in but a few steps, season to season could be but a nap.

The tin bucket sat on the ice-glossed front stoop. What a shock for Kate to have seen him freeze and then transform into hoar.

Checking his hands for flesh, Jal grimaced. Frost shape. Unacceptable to a frightened human woman.

Before he could knock, the door opened. He reached in quickly and touched Kate's cheek. His form took on human coloring and his body grew solid, shedding frost for flesh. Kate's expression tracked from stunned, to worried, to calm in a matter of blinks.

"Jal. You're looking…whole." She coughed, and her voice was raspy. "When you touch me, you…?"

"Take on mortal flesh and form. Can we talk?"

"I think that's a good idea."

She was acting rather calmly. A good thing. Unless the storm was waiting to rage. Females. They were very unpredictable. And no, he had not even begun to tread the surface of understanding them.

"Do you want me to get my coat so we can stand outside?" she asked.

"No, inside is good. I won't…"

"Melt?"

He wanted to touch her. To burn himself on her flesh. But he must be careful not to frighten her more than she may already be.

"So you saw everything," he said as he closed the door.

At the far wall a fire blazed. Kate paced before the end of the bed. She wore soft pink pants and a tight camisole with no bra. The jut of her nipples through the thin white fabric stirred him. Hell, he got a hard on.

Jal studied the missing window to keep from looking at Kate.

"Yes, I saw, well…" She coughed so roughly Jal felt the ache of her pain. "…a lot of freaky strange stuff."

"Your voice, Kate."

"It's a winter cold, or something. Like I said before, I don't feel sick, but my throat feels like I've been breathing icy air continually."

Like *his* air?

"Did you—" She stroked her throat. "Did *you* cause this?"

"I'm not sure, Kate. I'm sorry if I did. Please know I never told you my truths because, well, how does one go about saying they are the Frost god to a human woman?"

"So you *are* a god?" Her voice grew softer, the raspy affliction almost swallowing the tones. Her actions grew more disjointed, as if she was trying to understand, but her physicality wouldn't allow easy acceptance. "Not a faery?"

"That, too."

"A faery god?"

"I was born a changeling and was recruited into the folk—the lesser faery ranks—for the former Frost. Every thousand years a new Frost is chosen. Same with Ice and Snow."

"I see."

"Do you really?"

"Yes. No." She fisted delicate fingers near her ears and squeezed her eyelids shut. "I don't know. You've got to give me credit for not running from you screaming."

"That I do." He shuffled his feet and thought to walk

over to her, but perhaps he should let her come to him. "Kate, I…I'm not a monster."

"I don't believe in monsters."

"But you did once believe in snow queens."

"I did. I…still do."

"I was once mortal," he said softly. "I'm like you, at least my origins are. I…I can touch you without causing frostbite so long as I'm fleshed out."

"But when you're frost? Would a touch—"

"Deadly."

"I see." She grabbed a pink sweater from the end of the bed and put it on, tugging up the collar and rubbing it against her neck as if to sooth the ache. "Speaking of snow queens, what was that snow thing I saw you fighting out on my front yard? It looked…female."

"That was the Snow goddess. She's having a bad year. You shouldn't blame her for her anger. Ice calls it her cycle."

Kate smirked and hid a smile behind the sweater collar. "You're telling me the goddess of snow is having her period?"

"I don't know what that means, but she's been cranky and irritable for some time. She was the cause of the massive snowfall in your yard. And before that, I believe she was responsible for burying us out in the gorge. She's…angry with you, Kate."

"Me? Why?" Her voice cracked awkwardly. "Oh wait. Did I sleep with her boyfriend?"

"Who, me? Oh, no, Kate, I would never—well, we

can't, we Winter gods. It's just not done. And besides, she's not my type."

"Your type? Exactly what type does Jack Frost have?"

"My name's Jal, not Jack. And until I met you, the frost folk satisfied my needs."

"Those little things I saw on the front yard?"

"Yes, when thousands get together they can reform into one solid human shape, fitting for, well, you know."

"All righty then. So! I was satisfying a need for you? Like a cup of hot chocolate on a chilly afternoon?"

"No, Kate, our being together was much more than anything I've ever had or wanted. It was… That first day I saw you outside getting your mail, that's when this ache in my heart began to pulse."

"Getting my mail? I thought we met when I was taking pictures?"

"I saw you once before. I was…watching you. You were my mark. You came out that morning with your lacy pink underthings flashing brightly beneath the big parka. When you bent over I thought I'd never seen such a sweet sight."

She sat on the end of the bed and shrugged fingers through her hair. "You were checking out my ass?"

"It's like peaches and lace."

Kate bristled appreciatively. "So what do you mean I was your mark? What does *mark* mean? Is that like in the mafia movies when they talk about a— Oh, my God, Jal, were you…after me for a not-so-nice purpose? What did I read online…"

"I'm an assassin, Kate. I take my orders from Old

Man Winter. I touch environmental offenders and kill them with my frost."

A heavy swallow blocked Kate's throat. What he'd revealed, and so casually! "What kind of man are you? You sleep with the person you plan to then kill?"

"It's not like that, Kate."

"Then what is it like?"

"Like nothing I've ever known before. There was a mistake," he said softly. "I knew it the moment I saw you. I knew you couldn't possibly do harm to the world or any portion of it."

"I would never."

"So I had to discover the truth. I couldn't carry out my orders."

"But you've killed other mortals?"

He nodded. "It is what I am."

"I see."

Not only was Jack Frost the winter faery who could delight all ages with his frost designs, but indeed, his touch was deadly.

"But when you've touched me—"

"In this human form my touch does no harm. Only when I am frost."

"Then you look like those tiny bodies on my front yard?"

"My frost folk? You saw them?"

"I took pictures."

"They're faery, certainly. But I am *more*. I was once as they are; now I am a god. Can you accept me, Kate?"

"I, um…whew!" She stood, but then sat on the end

of the bed. "Accept you. A killer who delivers death by frostbite, yet can bring me to some kind of crazy wonderful with a mere kiss. I think it is your kisses that have given me this sore throat."

"I like you, Kate. I don't want to stop seeing you. But I'd understand if you wanted nothing to do with me. Maybe. I don't know. Feeling…it's very new to me."

She gestured for him to sit by her, and Jal crossed the room and settled next to her on the bed. She wanted him to kiss her. But if his kisses had made her ill, then what would prolonged exposure do to her?

"I know when I like a person and when I can trust him," she offered. "This sounds weird to say," she said, "but I have always felt something was missing in my life. That snow queen dream, you know? And then—now—a knight made of frost sweeps me off my feet and I'm feeling kind of fulfilled, like maybe something missing has finally been found. I want you in my life, Jal. But how will that work? I don't know if I can do this sore throat for much longer. And you, what effect do I have on you? Can I melt you?"

"We can have sex and touch and hold each other and I won't melt. I just need to go outside and cool off as soon after as I can."

"Is that why you were gone this morning? Because you needed to get cold?"

He nodded.

Okay, freak level should be off the scale, but Kate's strange calm reigned. Was it because the fantasy was too exquisite? That she wanted the impossible to work no matter what the price? Could she have a relationship with a man—*god*—who freely admitted he was an assassin?

"Kate, I have to tell you something. I am a god, and we don't have all the emotions you humans do. I lust, I get angry, but I never hunger, nor do I feel sympathy. That's an alien emotion I've only seen in the tears of children. And love, well, that's never been in my vocabulary. Until now."

He drew her hand over to his knee and held it. "Kate, I need you to know my truth. I love you. And I would die if I could not keep you safe."

"Can gods die?"

"We can all be destroyed. In whatever manner serves our bane." Such as laying his heart before her to melt? "You can't stay here in the northern states, Kate. You should go south where Snow can't get to you."

"You actually think she's going to try to do something to me?"

"She can, and she will."

"You told me you love me," she said. "But you also said you don't know what love is."

"I do now." And he leaned in to kiss her—and she let him.

Bittersweet, this kiss. For Kate sensed she could never enjoy it again, now knowing what she knew. Jal's breath cooled her throat, making her throat itch and she pushed him away.

"Am I too warm for you? Is your heart warm, Jal? Any part of you?"

"My heart is of frost, as I am. But I do feel warmth

spread through this human body. A dip in a snow bank is due. Have you family you can stay with? Far from the snow and ice and frost of this Minnesota winter?"

"My parents used to live in Florida."

"That's perfect."

"They've both passed, my mother just last year. Besides, I'm not going to let the abominable snowbitch scare me away."

"Kate, this is not a joke. The danger Snow presents is very real. Just for a few days? Take a vacation, fly south to the beach."

"I wish I did have parents to visit. We were never close." Kate sighed and looked to the side. "I was adopted twenty-four hours after my birth. My search for answers about my birth parents put my mother and I at odds."

"You were adopted? So these parents who recently passed, they were not your blood parents?"

"No, my real parents died in a car crash on the way to the hospital while my mother was in labor with me. I was the only survivor. Told you I have this weird ability to survive catastrophe."

A tiny ping sounded from the center of the living room. Kate stepped down from the bed to check her computer screen. Jal followed, looking over her shoulder at two digital photographs of snowflakes.

"Oh, my God," she said. "I've done it. Two snow-flakes. Exactly alike."

Chapter 11

"Are you sure?" Jal asked. Snowflakes could look very similar and yet be minutely different due to small imperfections or rime deposits. "Perhaps that's the same photograph, twice?"

Jal needn't argue. He knew the truth. Snow was bored; it didn't matter to her to create unique snowflakes. Truly, a new Snow goddess was needed.

And the one woman who could step up and take her place stood but a breath away. So unknowing. Yet so eager for the job according to dreams she'd had since childhood.

Kate couldn't be expected to sacrifice her cozy mortal life for that of a goddess. The very reason the gods were taken as newborns was so they were immediately acclimated, not forced to abandon a life, friends, family and perhaps a job. It is what made him so emotionless.

What *had* made him emotionless. Things had changed.

Jal wondered now about Kate being his mark. Had he taken her out that first day, she would have never made this discovery. Snow's secret would be safe.

"I've got to call Professor McClean." Kate reached for the phone. "This is worth a million dollars! Wait. I have to put together a presentation first. Yes, do this right, Kate. Don't jump into it until I've checked everything out. I've got to study all the points of delineation and recheck the computer's accuracy. Oh."

As if suddenly remembering Jal's presence, Kate turned and hesitantly touched his jaw.

"You've mastered what you set out to do," he said. A dip of his head nuzzled his cheek into her palm. "I should leave you to work. You're not angry with me for concealing my truth?"

She kissed him. The morsel touched the corner of his mouth, warming, threatening. For his heart pulsed hotly. Could he feel it melt?

"I love you, too," Kate whispered. "Can we make this work?"

"I'm not sure. This thing called love." He clasped a hand over his chest. There, it burned. "It is wondrous. Should a god be allowed such wonder? Is it not my bane to serve this world without its carnal rewards? I was once an unfeeling thing who did as he was told, to the benefit of your mortal realm. You've changed me, Kate."

She turned in his embrace and he wrapped an arm

around under her breasts. "It is a completely different realm where you come from, isn't it?"

"Nordika. And it is."

"Is it a world of snow and ice and frost?"

"As marvelous as Kate the snow queen can imagine."

"Will she come after me again? Now that I've found two matching snowflakes? That's why the snow goddess is angry with me, isn't it?"

"It is. But I will protect you, Kate. I promise. Snow is…not doing her job as it must be done according to the very law of nature. I have to leave you for a bit, but I promise I'll return. If you'll have me?"

"Of course I will. I'll wait for you tonight, outside."

"Will you hold off on reporting your find until after I've spoken to you again?"

She nodded and kissed him again.

"You saw the evidence?" Ice asked as he paced a thick snow-drifted glacier over the Arctic Sea.

Jal stood studying the blue wall of ice not a hundred yards away. The sea lashed up against the immense iceberg. The color of it was incredible. Ice did good work.

"Evidence. Yes, it was on her computer. She used the machine to detect similarities in various points on the snowflake, and it produced an exact match. But as I've told you, Snow has already confessed to making duplicates."

"Man, this cannot happen. She defies nature with her insolence! What is wrong with that goddess?"

"Perhaps…" The image of Snow stroking the red scarf came to him. No. Could she be? "I think she is in love."

"Love? With what? The abominable snowman? That chick is not in love. Nothing could love something so pestiferous in return."

And yet, Jal knew Kate had found it in her heart to love something not even mortal. Where there was a will, one in love would fall. "There's no question, a new Snow goddess is necessary. Kate's the one, Ice, the next Snow goddess."

"Your mortal fling?"

"Yes, and her blood parents died before she was born."

"That doesn't make sense. I thought the Universe tried but failed to kill her parents?"

"Her adopted parents. The real ones were in an accident on the way to the hospital. The adults were killed, and Kate was born through the miracle of medical intervention. The Universe was successful. Kate was orphaned *before* birth, but she was adopted less than twenty-four hours later. For some reason, the gods have always believed those to be her real parents."

"Then she could become Snow," Ice declared.

"Yes. Maybe. Would it not be impossible, mentally debilitating to ask her to shed her life for that of a god?"

"I don't know, man, this *is* a sweet life."

"You've nothing to compare it to. It is unlike the lives of mortals, that's sure. It is immense and powerful, and yet, we don't have things like hot chocolate and pink lace panties here."

"Pink lace? Frost, my man, you've really got it bad for her, don't you?"

"I told her I love her."

"You did not! Frost, you cannot afford emotion. It will be the death of you!"

"Too late, Ice." Jal smiled, and he felt it stretch deep into his heart. "I'd rather die than hide my true feelings from Kate again."

Winter had demanded an audience with Frost. And as the presence of the greatest season of all surrounded Frost, he began to question his actions. He'd done something wrong. He must accept the punishment.

And yet, acceptance did not mean he had to like it.

"Her discovery will devastate the mortal realm. You insolent!" Winter boomed.

"I don't understand how."

"It's…it's…" Never had Frost heard Winter struggle to form his thoughts. "The global warming thing."

"I don't buy that."

"Humans go mad over issues like that."

"Please, if they haven't panicked yet—and well they should be—two identical snowflakes is not going to push them over the edge."

"Yes, that is the pitiful truth. But there is also belief."

"Belief?"

"Yes, Vilhjalmur Frosti, what happens when the humans find out Frost is an assassin, the Snow goddess is a bored artist and Ice is a sex-crazed Lothario? Belief will be shattered. Myth, legend and lore will be altered. Humans rely on those things as staples in their history, why, their very existence! And I will not tolerate their belief being shattered."

Good points, all of them. But worth Kate's death? Never.

"There's more to this. Something you're not telling me."

"You don't need to know the reason. Do you forfeit your position as Frost god?"

"No."

"Then you will complete the task set to you before the night is dead!"

After a day spent leaning before the computer screen, Kate curved her body backward and stretched out her shoulders and spine. Whew, she hadn't realized how knotted up she had become sitting in one position for so long.

Everything checked out. The calculations and data point checks were all correct. She had found two identical snowflakes.

An amazing discovery she still shook her head over, but the data did not lie. And the pictures, she'd moved them over one another and tracked their points so many times she knew both snowflakes by heart. They were the same.

It was late, well past supper, so she would wait until tomorrow to call Professor McClean. Prolonging the moment would give her time to digest what had occurred.

She'd told Jal she would wait for him tonight, and she'd meant it.

"So you're going to date the Frost god?"

She smiled and nodded in agreement. Yet a fit of

coughs sent her rushing for the bathroom. "Need some humidity. Gotta kick this cold in the butt."

If only she weren't fooling herself. This was no cold. This was a result of breathing in Jal's kisses, it had to be.

Kate flicked on the shower to warm the room, then, the sight of the moon glinting on the small window made her shut off the water to stop the condensation.

There on the frost-covered window, he'd written: *I love you.*

And Kate started to cry, because she loved him, too. And what an impossible love.

A knock on the door lured her out to the living room. She wore a robe and underthings, and entirely expected Jal to be on the other side as she swung open the door.

Kate let out a chirp. It was not Jal, but instead, a tall woman with icy eyes and a crown of glittering snow-flakes dancing about her white hair.

Chapter 12

Kate hadn't chance to protest before the woman stepped inside and walked past her. A long white robe—hell, it was made of snow—flowed across the floor, the hem of it melting and staining the wood floorboards dark.

Dread crept up the back of Kate's neck. Would she get far if she ran? The goddess would laugh at the stupid human as she conjured something like a monster snowball to throw after her. Not on Kate's list of favorite ways to bite the big one.

"You must be Snow," Kate tried. Her raspy voice wavered uneasily. *Get it together, girl.* Jal said he'd protect her. Would he arrive soon? Like, now!

"Kate Wilson." The goddess hooked her hands at her hips. She stood in fleshed human form and wore mortal clothing—of snow. Fashion-model bone structure and a sexy white slip of a dress hugged long pale legs. She radiated all colors and exhaled gorgeous silver breath. "Not at all charmed to meet you."

Jal had been right about the PMSing goddess. Crabby for an entire year? Kate could be thankful she was only grumpy once a month.

Well, if she had come to kill her, Kate had no intention of going down without a fight. "What do you want?"

"I like a woman who gets right to it. Points for you, Kate Wilson."

The goddess strolled the length of the sofa and wandered before the computer desk. "What's that?" She pointed to the printouts and photographs of the snowflakes Kate had slaved over all afternoon.

"Field work," Kate offered. "I'm a snowflakologist."

"Uhuh." The goddess leaned over the images. Flakes fell from her hair and dusted the dry paper.

Kate cringed. The melting snowflakes would ruin the printouts. But she had all her work backed up on disk.

"Looks like you've found out my secret." Snow trailed a finger along Kate's work. "I could destroy it all."

"You c-could." A cough was imminent, but she held it back out of fear.

"Or I could give you this boon in exchange for your help."

"My help?"

Not for one moment did Kate believe the goddess had a compassionate flake in her body. And yet, they were both women. She could relate to her frustrations, surely.

So she'd become bored with creating snowflakes? What woman wasn't allowed a little respite every once in a while? Especially with a job so tedious.

No, creating snowflakes could not be boring. It must be the most wondrous job ever.

Snow approached. Kate stepped back, but the sofa behind her stopped her retreat.

"You're lovely," Snow said. "A determined woman, am I correct?"

"I take pride in my work. I love a good challenge." And even while shaking at standing before this goddess who had tried to kill her, she meant that statement as a thrown gauntlet.

The cool touch of the woman's finger traced Kate's jaw. Not so cold as Jal's touches, and softer, as if kissed by winter.

"Winter gods are not meant to love the warm-blooded," Snow said.

She knew? Had Jal told her?

"Frost's heart grows dangerously warm," she continued. "You will kill him if you continue to allow him to love you."

"Don't gods have free will?"

"We do."

"Then I can't be the one to tell Jal how to feel."

"Feelings. Emotion. Love. That is what threatens your lover. Do you want the world to suddenly be without frost?"

"Well, no, but frost isn't everywhere. The tropics—"

"Insolent," the snow goddess hissed. "You're a smart

woman, Kate. Think. Frost has never known love until you. First loves are...quite spectacular. One does not think rationally. They do things detrimental to their well-being. They rush blindly toward the unknown. Do you really want to kill him?"

"K-kill him? No," Kate breathed out. Her love could really—

"Then release him from your harmful love. Break his heart. Send him away. Restore balance to the world, Kate Wilson. It is in your hands."

Kate exhaled heavily.

"Do so and I will allow you your silly photographs. No one will believe you anyway. Those fancy machines are designed to replicate lies and the data to back up such falsities. Can I trust you'll do as I ask?"

The cool aura wavering off the goddess tickled a shiver over Kate's arms. If she did not do as asked, she felt very sure the goddess would not only destroy her research, but her, as well.

Her love was killing Jal? His heart, which must be cold, was warming to feel such an emotion. And a warm heart in a man made of frost could not be a good thing.

Kate nodded. "I never thought about Jal's impact on the world. Or what could happen if he began to love a human. I'll send him away. I'll...stop loving him. I have to. I promise."

"Good girl."

And the goddess swirled into a storm of snow. The front door opened, and the storm whisked through.

* * *

The printouts were soggy. Kate lifted them carefully. The ink had smeared from the goddess's touch.

"She's right. You have goals, dreams. You want that million dollars so you can travel the world. Who has time for a boyfriend?" A swallow cut like razors inside her throat. "And what a fool to think I could make a go of it with a man made of frost."

She reached for the phone receiver but didn't lift it from the cradle. The professor's number was on speed dial. Whatever he wanted to do with the results was out of her hands. He could publish it in a science journal or plaster it across the headlines of the *New York Times* for all she cared.

Really?

Her niggling conscience made her release the phone. Kate sucked in the corner of her lower lip. "If the world knows two identical snowflakes exist, then…"

She'd only wanted people to believe in her, and in the world as she saw it. But by publishing her discovery… Could belief be threatened?

It was a weird thing to consider, but the results *could* devastate. Childhood dreams would be crushed. The belief in the magical, that out of all the uncountable number of snowflakes in the world not one was the same—it must be protected. If not, people would become disenchanted with winter.

Kate knew her finding was an anomaly only because the Snow goddess admitted to making copies. Explain that one to the world.

"I can't do this," she whispered. "I can't take money because the Snow goddess is bored. I need to make things right. I need to…"

For starters, she had to break it off with Jal.

How to kill a woman he loved?

He had his orders. They were to be taken seriously. And now he knew Kate's discovery could prove cataclysmic to the world. Should she announce her find, the repercussions would move through the mortal world as if dominos clacking across the divide.

She had to be stopped. And he was the assassin to do it.

"No!" Too late, he had fallen in love. No longer could he dispassionately give death to a mortal. Was he finished as Frost?

Did he care? Because to be with Kate…

There was another option. And for the first time, Jal desperately wanted options. If he could destroy Kate's research then he would not have to destroy her.

"Selfish," Jal muttered as he paced the road before Kate's house. "Do I wish this for my benefit? The current Snow goddess can survive another thousand years."

And yet, his heart pleaded for options. A fighting chance to be with the woman he loved.

"I must at least explain things to Kate. Reveal her destiny. Oh."

He clutched his chest. It did not so much ache now as bleed. Blood did not flow in the gods' veins. Should he take human form, ichor would ooze from his heart. Had she warmed him beyond all hope?

No, it was emotion, an intangible brand of contact that would bring his end. He'd confessed his love. It felt splendid. And it hurt.

But if his chest cracked open and his insides melted upon the ground today, it would have been worth it for the brief time he'd had with Kate.

"What have you done to me, Kate? You've…changed me. Shown me happiness. I don't want to destroy, I simply want to sustain."

Striding up the drive, Jal held up his hand as a breeze whisked a sparkling powder of crystals from the rooftop. Snow folk. They landed on his palm—and he crushed them.

"Snow will not harm Kate. If I must surround this cabin with my own folk and build a fierce wall of rime to keep back Snow's army, I shall."

Kate stood in the doorway, bundled in a dark turtle-neck sweater and matching pants. She didn't waver or protest when Jal—formed of frost—reached to kiss her cheek. Human flesh and clothing glamorized his form.

"Going out?" he asked.

"No. You're incredible in your natural frost form, Jal. So beautiful."

"I usually brush against your flesh and change so quickly you don't register it. I didn't want to frighten you before."

"And now?"

Her voice was tiny and sore, bruised by his icy kisses.

He felt her pain tangibly. He had harmed her? But love was not supposed to hurt, was it?

"There are many truths you must have, Kate. Might I come inside?"

"Yes, of course. Over by the hearth? I didn't light a fire."

"That's why you're dressed so warmly. I thank you for your consideration."

She kissed him, but quickly, and at only the corner of his mouth.

"Is something wrong, Kate?"

Of course something was wrong. She had just kissed the man who was supposed to kill her.

It was easier to stand and distance herself from Jal than to sit close to him. Close enough to kiss. Close enough to forget she was killing him.

She was *killing* him.

Each time he returned to her his heart grew warmer. Did he not realize that? Or did he, and yet, not care?

She would not be responsible for harming a god who served the world, why, who made it beautiful with his creations, and yes, even warned and sometimes killed with his touch. It was the way of nature. Vilhjalmur Frosti *was* nature. Before she'd known what he was, she had seen him for what he truly was, but simply wasn't willing to believe her eyes.

Now she knew how her parents had felt when they'd tried to understand her odd manner of seeing the world. It's easier to not believe than to accept what might be standing right before you.

"This isn't working," she said abruptly.

Jal stood and reached for her, but she turned to pace before the hearth. Should have lit a fire, a safe zone to flee to from her lover's disappointed stare.

"I've given it a lot of thought. All night, in fact."

Kate crossed her arms over her chest. Most of those thoughts had been sexy images of she and Jal entwined on the bed. They had only made love once. It wasn't enough. She wanted him. Always. But it wasn't meant to be. "I don't want you to come here ever again."

"What are you saying? You don't—"

"I can't love you," she enunciated firmly. *And please don't argue with me, because I can't do this either.* His hurt expression stabbed her. "We're not even the same species. This is so wrong, Jal. Besides, my throat hurts so much." She forced a sniffle.

"Kate?" He moved so quickly, she tried to back away from the imminent embrace, but before she knew it, Jal held her in his arms. "You're shivering."

"I'm upset. And you're—" cruel to say it "—cold!"

Kate pushed him away from the embrace that threatened to change her mind, and crossed to the door. Holding it open, a gush of chilly air brushed her shoulders. Like Jal's kiss. But his kisses had never chilled her so dreadfully as this conversation. He wasn't cold at heart. And that was the problem. Warm heart; death sentence.

"Please leave, Jal. Don't make this harder than it has to be."

He walked slowly across the room, his eyes not

meeting hers. His fingertips traced the top of the couch, retracting, then touching the soft yarn on her pink mitten.

"Kate?"

Lowering her head, she looked aside, unable to meet those incredible ice blue eyes and his sad kicked puppydog expression.

"I will always love you," he whispered.

No, please no, she thought. It will kill you.

And when she couldn't stand it any longer, Kate gasped back the tears and turned to embrace her lover.

But he wasn't there.

Fresh snow swirled in from the open doorway. Moonlight shimmered across the packed snow, dancing in the wings and limbs of Frost's fallen folk.

And Kate could no longer hold back the tears.

He stumbled across the drive, clutching his chest. It bled copiously now. And the ichor was not ice cold but hot, thick and deadly. Tripping forward, Jal caught himself in the snow where his own folk had battled fiercely against the snow goddess.

He clutched the pink mitten, rubbing the warmth of it aside his cheek. One last touch of Kate.

Taking on the crystals of his fallen folk, his body transformed to frost—all, save his weeping heart.

Chapter 13

Kate dropped the pine log in the snow. She kicked it, and then kicked at the snow bank.

She plopped down on the bank and threw back her arms to land on the powdery snow. Moonglow dazzled the midnight landscape. Snowflakes fell noisily, their crystals clicking on the cottonwood branches and skittering across the sparkling surface of snow around her.

The seductive winter illumination boldly toyed with her need to be angry, to want to kick and shout and scream.

She'd made her lover leave—by lying to him.

"To save him," she whispered.

Denying her heart was something she'd never consciously done before. Yet, to think on it, she'd denied herself relationships for years by moving out here to the cabin.

And oh, did it hurt. How cruel to send Jal away with a few brisk words. The look in his eyes had reached in and crushed her heart. She had been his only experience with love. And look what she'd done with that fragile, new emotion.

"Oh, Kate, you've done a bad thing."

And yet, it could only be bad for her. The world needed Vilhjalmur Frosti. She mustn't be selfish.

A kiss of snow dusted her cheeks and nose. The flakes melted and teared down her flesh.

"Well done," a female voice said.

Kate's heart shuddered, but then she exhaled to release the apprehension. "He won't die now?" she asked the Snow goddess who stood just out of sight behind her. "His heart will grow cold again, and Frost will live?"

"That's not what I've come to discuss."

"I need to know!"

"Sure." Prickling snow crystals sifted across Kate's face. "My thanks for not revealing the snowflake copies to the world. It could have proven catastrophic in ways mere humans cannot begin to imagine."

"Loss of enchantment," Kate muttered, "loss of belief, of wonder. I can understand."

Whoopee for her, she'd saved the world. So why did she feel so miserable?

Kate leaned forward. To her side the goddess, in human form, sat upon the snow bank, her weight not crushing a single flake. Knee-high white boots and a tight-fitted skirt and shirt exposed bare arms glittering with flakes. Long hair spilled past her hips and sifted flakes onto Kate's leg.

"What do you want now?" Kate leaned back against the snow chair formed by her body. "To kill me?"

The goddess flicked her fingers, dispersing flakes through the air. "Not at the moment."

"Great. I've sent away the man I love, and now I have to live with it."

"But you saved the world."

"Joy."

"You humans are difficult to please. Whatever. I am little disturbed by your heartbreak." The goddess leaned an elbow on the snow. She touched a strand of Kate's hair and shivered. "Humans, so warm."

"Can I kill you with my warmth?"

"Do you want to?"

Kate sighed. "Not so much."

This whole experience had worn her ragged. She didn't want to harm anyone, god or faery or whatever the heck they called themselves. Especially not after she'd seen the look in Jal's eyes.

"I've a proposal for you," Snow offered.

"Swell." Kate tugged her hair from the goddess's playful touch.

"I wonder if you're interested in taking my job?"

"Your job? You mean, Snow goddess?" What the hell?

And in her next thought, Kate's mind zoomed to the childhood dream of being snow queen. Yes! She could create snow and blanket the world with her gorgeous white crystals, and—

No. A human become a goddess? The offer was too bizarre.

"Now you're teasing me, and I'm not sure what for."

"It's not a tease." Snow leaned back on her elbows. Lashes resembling fernlike branches on a snowflake blinked over her cold white eyes. "Obviously Frost didn't let you in on your secret."

"My secret? It doesn't work that way, lady. If I have a secret I'd have to let Jal in on it."

"So why didn't you tell him you were the snow goddess changeling?"

"The what?"

"You see? Just close your mouth and listen, human. These are the details. I learned from Ice about your adoption."

"That happened twenty-eight years ago. My real parents died before I was even born."

"Yes, well, none of the gods were aware of that switcheroo. We always believed the adopted pair your blood parents. If we had known your real parents had died—well, I wouldn't be talking to you right now. Or rather I would be, while I was training you."

"You are talking in code."

"You were born into this world a changeling, Kate Wilson. A snow faery."

Kate sat upright and twisted on her snow seat to better eye the goddess. "Like those little bodies I found littered all over my yard yesterday? I'm not—no, that's not right."

Snow blew out a breath of snow crystals that lingered in the air before her. They began to dance about, and Kate knew they were snow folk, tiny beings with wings and designed of ice crystals. It was not even dreadful to admire their magical dance swirling high into the air until they dispersed over the treetops.

"Every thousand years a new changeling is born into the mortal realm," Snow explained. "The parents are immediately disposed of and the child is taken to be trained for their future task as Snow god. Or Frost god. Or Ice, whichever. The gods tried to kill your adopted parents—not knowing the real ones were already dead—three times."

"I—I know that," Kate gasped. "We've always had the family joke we can survive even the craziest of situations. That was the gods? And me, I'm…"

"You should have been my replacement."

"That makes so much sense."

"It does?"

Struck silent, Kate could merely nod, and the tiniest of grins curled her mouth. That certainly explained the way she saw nature. Because…she was a part of it, too?

"Good, then I'm going to cut to the chase. I want you to take over my job. I'm tired of it. And besides, I have *things* waiting for me. Places to be. So you'll do it?"

"Just like that? Become made of snow and ice crystals and— But how?"

"It's a god thing."

"To be like you…" Composed entirely of snow? To

live somewhere only the gods lived? What had Jal call it? Nordika.

It was too overwhelming to fathom. And yet, Kate's heart raced not out of fear, but with excitement. Because if she became a goddess, then she would be the same as—

"Can I be with Jal if I become the Snow goddess?"

"Sure," Snow purred. "Once cold ichor fills your veins, you can share your life with Frost, and make love to him and help him spread winter across the land. It's what you were born to be, Kate."

"I'll do it. If I can be with Jal. And—just yes."

"Splendid."

The snow swirled into a land funnel and Snow glimmered out of sight.

Kate turned and propped her elbows on the snow and followed the tendril of spinning dazzle high into the midnight sky.

"I've always known," she murmured.

Jal landed on Ice's doorstep. Hoar and rime crystals deformed his torso. Ice water dripped down his thighs, freezing the frost and in places melting it into painful ice.

He gathered all his energy to reform and knock on the door.

An ice faery answered. Her clear ice nipples jutted suggestively. Jal stepped inside, uninterested in the naked faery. Flakes of hoar fluttered from his form with each step.

"Ice!" the faery screamed and directed Frost toward

the frozen sofa, without touching him. "Hurry up, your friend is in a bad way."

Ice slid across the skating rink floor and landed on the sofa next to Jal's. He reached over and plucked a crumbling chunk of hoar from Jal's knee.

"What in the Arctic Ocean? What's up with you, man?"

"She…" Jal shuddered. A few crystals fell from his jaw. Here in Ice's palace he knew the means to survive would be greater. He sucked in the cool icy air to reform his dwindling shape. "…doesn't love me."

"Oh, hell no, Frost, don't let this happen. Every thought you have about the human is one step closer to your death. You're feeling! Stop it!"

"Can't. Love…h-her."

Ice directed the faery away. He held his crystal clear hands before Jal, unsure or maybe deciding what he could do to help. A touch to Jal's arm hardened his crystals and allowed Jal to sit upright.

"That'll help for a bit," Ice said. "But you're dying, man. Snap out of it. Don't let that human do this to you."

"I will die…h-happily…for having known…"

"Don't say it, just don't. I'm going down there to talk to that woman."

A gust of frigid wind froze Jal to the sofa. It was a good thing—but not for long.

Ice slid along the shores of Greenland, when he sighted Snow and the mortal woman.

"What the hell is *she* doing here?" he shouted at the Snow goddess.

"You must be Ice," the mortal said, far too accepting of a man shaped of ice for his comfort. "You're a friend of Jal's."

"And you broke his heart, you nasty—"

Snow grabbed the mortal's hand, but Ice was not finished. "She's killed him!"

"What?" The mortal tugged out of Snow's grip. Though bundled in snow gear, her cheeks showed signs of frostbite. The red circles at the centers of her cheeks were turning white and waxy. "But she said if I broke Jal's heart, it would grow cold again."

"Oh, did she?" Ice turned to Snow, who delivered a cocky sneer. "You knew he was in love. The man can't turn off the emotion and harden his heart. It's completely melted. He's going down fast."

"Too bad." Snow grabbed Kate's hand and whisked them into a whirl of snow. "If I can't have my lover, Frost won't have his."

Kate stumbled over hard, iced snow chunks in the goddess's wake. She had no idea where Ice had gone. But what he'd said. Frost's heart was still melting? "But you said Jal and I could be together."

"I lied. I've no power to make you a goddess. That is Old Man Winter's boon. But you remain a deterrence to my next replacement. I must remove that deterrent."

Kate inspected the goddess's pale eyes. There was no determining if she spoke truth or was lying. But what reason had she to lie? If only Jal were here.

You sent him away. You killed him.

"Stupid human." The goddess gripped Kate's arm. "Keep your eyes closed."

"But why—" A gust of ice crystals blew roughly across Kate's face, like sandpaper of ice. She pressed her gloved hands over her eyes.

The twosome lifted into the air, and the world slipped away. Kate's body soared weightlessly forward. Though she wore her good Arctic Cat snow wear, bracing wind curled around Kate's neck and down her spine.

"Keep 'em closed," Snow said. "We're here."

"Where's here?" Kate shouted because the wind whistled loudly. "Is it storming?"

"Not yet. It's a beautiful sunny day here on top of Everest."

Everest? Kate wasn't prepared to stand atop Everest. That required oxygen and sunglasses and more clothing than she was wearing.

"Thanks for tricks, Kate Wilson."

And the goddess let go of Kate's arm. Kate wobbled, knowing she had to keep her hands over her eyes. To open them would risk burning her corneas, snowblindness would quickly follow.

"She said something about you not having your lover if she couldn't have hers. I didn't know Snow had a thing going on."

"But I told you before—" The pink mitten Jal still held made him consider. "The red scarf."

"What?"

Jal reached out to touch Ice. The chill contact seeped

through his melting crystals and hardened them. But each time he refroze the melting crystals, his shape became more distorted. "The mortal object, it was a scarf. Snow was fixated on it when I visited her. It's like this mitten.

"From her lover?"

"Possibly."

"That would explain her urgency to lose the job. Bitch. So she's going to punish you, but then she'll be changed to a mortal and she can go shack up with her human lover."

"I don't think Old Man Winter will let it happen," Jal said. "He's the only one who can make Kate a goddess. Snow's got Kate?"

Ice nodded. "Ran into them off the coast of Greenland, but she's headed northeast, I'm sure."

"I've got to find her. Kate's not safe."

"Take this with you." Ice handed Jal a shard of ice. "It'll keep you cold enough, I hope."

Frost clutched the icicle. It permeated his system, hardening the melting portions and sent out tendrils of fernlike frost all over.

He couldn't stop his heart from melting. There was no going back, no changing his thoughts to what they'd been those few moments before he'd met Kate. She was a part of him now. He carried her smile in his heart. Even though that same smile had straightened, and had denied him love.

If she could stop loving him, wasn't it possible he could do the same?

But he didn't want to. The wondrous emotion was all that he had.

"I'll go talk to Old Man Winter," Ice said. "You go rescue the girl."

"I'm on it."

Frost stood, and his legs shattered, dropping him in a pile of crisp crystals. At that instant a sweep of brisk air coiled about him, reforming his crystals, and bringing him to stand upright. But he wasn't doing this. Jal could but wonder at his sudden return of strength.

"You've a new mark," Old Man Winter's voice vibrated in all of Jal's crystals. "In Iceland. I've the coordinates—"

"No!" No marks now. Nothing mattered but saving Kate. "Kate is in trouble. She needs me."

"The mortal photographer? You defy me, Frost."

"I do not wish to, my liege. But right now a mortal's life is at stake."

"Another mortal's life must be extinguished! If you refuse this task, Frost, then you forfeit your job. You will no longer be a Winter god!"

Winter left in a fierce storm that obliterated the room Jal stood in and left him out in the open air, standing atop a glistening rise of snow crystals. Snow stretched as far as he could see. Gorgeous, glittering. His home, here in Nordika.

No longer a winter god? The thought disturbed him. "But Kate." He clutched his chest where the warming sensation had not ceased.

She doesn't love you. Do not sacrifice your job for a mere mortal.

The memory of her kiss, sweet upon his lips, could never be erased.

Chapter 14

Ice waited a long time for Old Man Winter to show. When he finally did, Ice sensed tension in the god's presence. But, determined to help a friend, he explained Snow's devious plays against Frost and Kate to Old Man Winter. Together, the two of them tracked the human man Snow had been having an affair with, an Alaskan truck driver.

The affair with a mortal did not disturb Old Man Winter so much as that Snow had set out to murder a mortal only for the reason that she would then be released from her job. He was outraged his gods would harbor such foul deeds under his very nose. Juneau experienced a freak snowstorm as a result. No lives were lost, but the city was brought to a silent standstill for three days.

"I'll have to find a new changeling within the day," Old Man Winter growled.

"But there's Kate Wilson," Ice suggested. "She was born to be Snow. Put her on the fast track to becoming a goddess, and she may be able to save Frost."

"Frost will choose his own destiny. And I do not wager in love, underling."

"Of course you do." Ice slid across the rink that formed before him. A twirl and masterful jump displayed the whimsical wintertime activity lovers shared. "Winter is the most romantic time of the year. Couples fall in love in the winter all the time. Ice-skating in Central Park. Snowball fights that result in laughter and snuggling before a cozy fire. Ice storms that strand young lovers in an out-of-the-way hotel. Chilly kisses under pine trees that shower snow crystals over their wool-capped heads."

"Perhaps."

"That's the spirit!" Not really, but Ice was working against the clock, so he had to appeal to the Winter god's ego because there was no compassion in the master god's form.

"Kate is missing. Snow took her somewhere; she may have killed her. Frost is searching for her. What can you do about this?"

"For romance?" Winter grumbled.

Ice nodded eagerly.

Old Man Winter's heavy sigh blasted snow and crystals over Ice's frozen body. Felt great.

The Winter god declared, "Kate Wilson is Snow, as I command."

"Right now?"

Old Man Winter shrugged. "She needs to stand before me for the transformation to occur."

"Great!" Ice turned to skate off, but paused and glanced over a shoulder. "What about the former Snow?"

"She is granted mortality, as is our way."

"And her lover?"

"He—" Old Man Winter said with a glint to his icy voice "—has suddenly developed an interest in tropical climes."

Ice bowed gratefully. "Thanks, my liege."

No job was more important than the life of another.

Jal knew the one spot in the entire mortal world Snow frequented most. He went there often, himself. All the Winter gods convened at Everest; it was the one mortal place fit for them.

But it was not fit for humans. If Snow had taken Kate there—

In a fog of frost, he glided off from Nordika and aimed for the world's highest mountain peak. The sun was cold and cruel, glittering across the deadly mountain with deceptive invitation—a summons Jal admired.

He spied a train of mortals hiking up toward what he knew was called Base Camp 3. One more stop before the hikers would require oxygen. Most would not make it to the peak. Today the four men and their sherpas would be successful, for Frost had not a mark.

But they'd never make it there to see what Jal saw. A small figure heaped over on the top of Everest.

Kate.

Dispersing, Jal fell swiftly to ground, his crystals gathering on the snow pack near Kate's face. But he was yet weak. His heart still bled.

"She said she didn't love me."

Half-formed, Frost clutched at his dripping heart. Hoar crystals clattered as his fingers scraped over them and dropped onto Kate's exposed cheek. A cheek white with frostbite.

"Not from me," he muttered. "I would never, Kate. I love you. I always will."

It mattered not what she thought of him, that she could not love him. Of course she could not. He asked far too much of a human. But he would not allow her to die for having once loved him.

He touched her cheek. No warmth. His frost form did not assume flesh.

A fierce wind razored the air, tearing apart Jal's structure and scattering him across the snow and over Kate's body.

Something moaned. She was alive. Not for long.

Jal focused and called on his folk. The air glittered with dancing frost folk. He commanded them to him and minute crystal structures bonded with his, forming, shaping, making him whole, until he sat beside Kate, his legs stretched out before him. He held a hand before his face, watching as the last two fingers formed.

Another moan alerted him. Jal twisted and tugged at Kate's coat. He had to work fast, or his melting heart would see him decimated. He plunged a hand inside her coat and up under her shirt.

"So cold."

But there, between her breasts, the tiniest pulse of warmth imbued his crystals. Kate's last remnant of body heat moved through him, giving him solid form and human flesh. Fully formed, Jal gasped at the lacking oxygen and brisk cold.

She moaned as he lifted her into his arms.

"Don't open your eyes, Kate. It's Jal."

Now what to do? He couldn't descend the mountain and deposit her at the base camp. He'd never make it that far. Kate hadn't enough body heat to keep him in human form. He'd change to frost and she would fall through his grasp.

"Jal?"

"Quiet. Save your breath. I love you, Kate, even if you cannot love me."

"But…I…"

He shushed her. "Never forget that. I love you."

He looked about, scanning the vast horizon. The sun burned his human eyes. Perhaps this is how it would be from now on. He'd defied Old Man Winter by refusing to go after the mark.

So would he die here on Everest as punishment?

Not before he saw Kate safe.

Jal lifted Kate high in his arms and called out to Old Man Winter, "I have her! She is here. The Snow goddess!"

Chapter 15

Ten months later...

Jal finished off a letter to the editor at Stellar Publishing. He'd spent the week looking through the photographic galleys for the book he'd pieced together from Kate's snowflake photographs. It was ready to go to press.

He plunked out the last few letters, cursing his fear of taking one of those online typing classes. Hunt-and-peck worked fine enough for the little typing he did. He was slow to embrace the electronics in this little cabin. It had proved wonder enough just walking through the spring and summer months, learning all the foliage and weather and human foibles.

He'd survive. Had to. This human experience would

not defeat him. It was growing on him, actually. But the emotion part was quite a wallop.

Shutting off the computer, he then noticed something wondrous through the front window.

"Snow." He rushed to the door, bare feet tramping the scattered clothes he never could get accustomed to hanging up after use.

Drawing open the door, stirred in a swirl of thick cotton-puff flakes. Winter's kiss gave Jal a chuckle. He stepped out onto the stoop, already thick with snow and gave a whoop at the chill of it. He stepped back inside and made a beeline for the closet where he'd stored winter gear in anticipation of just this moment.

"So cold," he said gleefully as he pulled on winter boots and jacket. "I never imagined it could be like that."

He straightened. The things he caught himself saying. No longer a god, he was completely mortal, and had grown to adore the heat of the sun on his bare shoulders and face. Yet, always, he pined for winter.

And it had arrived. His first winter as a human.

Sweeping a scarf about his neck, Jal tugged on a ski cap as he dashed outside, leaving the front door wide open. It was late, but moonlight sparkled across the thin expanse of snow. Thick flakes landed on the sleeve of his jacket and he brought up his arm to delight at the crystals.

Squinting, he tried to see the shapes of snow folk mixed within the flakes, but the flakes were simply white, glittery clumps. He could no longer see the depth, the color and various branches and formations his Frost god eyes had seen.

But no matter. Jal licked the thick clump of flakes from his sleeve. Such delight! Snow!

He rushed through the yard, seeking the silvery band that glittered between the spacing of the trees. "It is magnificent!"

He had not felt so carefree for months. Missing winter as he had, missing *her*. Could there be a chance—

But of course—he held up his palm, catching the snowflakes—this must be her work.

A soft wind soughed through the tree branches, moving the falling flakes in a sudden dodge to the left. Jal turned and there, in the center of the yard, where the moon spotlighted the new snow, the crystals began to swirl and rise.

Brilliant cold moonlight danced in the coil. It began to form, to sweep in falling snowflakes, and soon the hands caressed the air, moving up along the figure as if directing snow folk to position.

When completed, Jal could but gasp. Never had he looked upon so gorgeous a sight. Not even in all his centuries as a god. His heart pulsed and speeded. That initial ache he'd first felt when spying her last winter returned. He reached out, but then snapped back his hand to clutch at his chest.

And she approached, every step stirring and swirling the flakes and glinting crystals that designed the gown hugging her legs and torso.

Had he dreamed of this moment? Or had his every waking moment been but steps, moves and pining closer to her presence?

Did she remember him? Could she?

Jal had thought he'd forgotten the scent of winter, of crisp, brisk cold so perfect it made his insides stir. Now it approached and as the Snow goddess stopped before him, he felt the hot touch of a tear slip down his cheek.

"Kate?"

The Snow goddess smiled and reached to touch his cheek, just shy of the tear trail. Jal's warmth permeated her snow crystals, rushing over snow flesh and forming human skin and features and hair. And Kate's spring green eyes.

A spill of frothy white fabric skimmed to her ankles. The Snow goddess had come home.

"I've been waiting for first snow," she said. Grasping the ends of Jal's scarf, she stepped closer, a little tentative. "You sacrificed your life for me."

"I've still a human life. We could have never been together if we were both gods."

"Not cool to mix snow and frost." She smirked. "But snow and mortal flesh?"

"So long as you cool down if you get too warm."

"Oh, lover."

Her lips were cool, and that made Jal smile against her mouth. He pulled her close, shivering as their flesh touched and her body limned to his. "I've hot chocolate," he whispered against her silky hair. "Let me go ahead inside and put out the fire, yes?"

She unzipped his jacket. A cold hand to his abdomen made him jump, yet again, he could only smile. "So that's how it's to be?"

"Right here." She shed the silky dress with a shimmy of her shoulders and hips. "Right now."

"What if I get frostbite?"

"I don't bite, Jal. Unless you want me to."

* * * * *

ICE BOUND
Vivi Anna

Dear Reader,

I love mythology. Any type from any culture. The way people use stories to make sense of what is happening around them fascinates me.

When Michele asked me if I wanted to do this duet of winter-inspired stories with her, I was immediately excited. I knew I could incorporate some interesting mythology into it. I searched different texts for winter-based deities or myths, and found one from Japan. The story about Yuki-Onna, the snow woman.

I was intrigued by the tale and knew instantly it would work for the story I had in mind. I changed a few details and added my own background for her, but in the end it is still about a ghostly woman in a kimono who comes to those stranded in the snow.

I hope you enjoy "Ice Bound." It was refreshing to write it.

All my best,

Vivi Anna
Visit me at www.vivianna.net.

For Kim. My BFF in every sense.

Chapter 1

Beneath the steel hull of the *Aurora* ship, the sound of ice cracking broke the eerie silence of the frozen landscape. Leaning over the side of the boat, Dr. Darien Calder watched as the boat cut a path through the ice. Twenty years ago, the ship would've had difficulty getting through the sea ice shelf, but after years of global warming, it didn't take much to break the frozen topography.

That was why he was here in Hokkaido, Japan, floating in a ship in the middle of an ice shelf—to observe and record the transformation in the environment.

He was also there to learn more about a legend that had haunted him, had invaded his dreams nightly, from the moment he learned of it—the legend of Koori-Onna. It told of a beautiful, ghostly woman appearing to lost travelers in snowstorms, who with one kiss from her icy lips literally froze the doomed victim from the inside out.

Every culture had a similar myth. The Ice Princess, the Snow Queen. But for some reason this one stood out to him.

Although he was a scientist, there was something about the story that resonated with him, something that moved past his analytical side and captured his imagination. Since arriving in Japan, his dreams had become more vivid, more stirring. He'd awoken twice now in a cold sweat, a tingling sensation lingering on his lips. But for now, he was here to study the ice flow and do the job he was paid to do. Not to fantasize about a legend.

The drifting ice was having a hell of an effect on the climate conditions in the area. Because the freezing process removed salt from the water, when it melted, as it had been doing in record amounts, it changed the water from salt to fresh water. At the rate things were changing, it wouldn't be long before the surrounding wildlife was irrevocably affected. Darien sighed. It was his job to make sure that didn't happen.

"What do you think?"

Darien looked over at Jiro Noda, the local scientist he'd been e-mailing for the past five months, and nodded. Over the months they had formed a friendship. "The ice levels are definitely thinning."

"And it is early yet." Jiro motioned toward the shelf with the sweep of his hand. "It is only December, and the flow is moving already. We usually do not see this until mid-January."

"Climate shifts have taken place all over the world." Darien glanced down into the dark water beneath the boat. "I sense a major shift coming. Maybe the poles are really going to switch."

Jiro simply lifted a dark brow in answer, as if he didn't have the words to equal Darien's statement. "God, I really hope not."

The thought scared Darien, too. He could imagine the disasters that would follow if magnetic north all of a sudden became magnetic south. He wasn't sure if the earth would survive that. Or not so much the earth, as the people living on its surface.

Resigned to their individual thoughts, Darien and Jiro spent another three hours out in the water, checking and measuring the thickness of the ice shelf. By the time the ship docked, the tips of Darien's fingers were beginning to throb from the bitter cold. Frost had formed on the stubble along his jaw. He imagined he looked like a young version of Old Man Winter.

After the crew tied off the boat, Jiro and Darien carried the equipment to shore and stored it in Darien's rented SUV. His plan was to drive back to Kushiro, where he had rented the vehicle, and catch a small plane back to Sapporo, and from there continue to Tokyo. However much he appreciated the icy beauty of the north, he really wanted to get back to the main city and play tourist for a few days before heading back to America.

Glancing up into the hazy sky, he figured he still had about five good hours to make the two-hour trip. As long as it didn't snow, he'd be fine on the usually hazardous roads. Winter driving in Japan was sometimes considered a contact sport—slipping and sliding on the awful roads while trying desperately not to hit an oncoming vehicle.

With the equipment tightly packed, Darien offered his hand to the other man. "It was good working with you, Jiro. I hope to see you again soon."

Jiro took his hand and shook it firmly. "I packed that tent I told you about in the back. I think it will be good for your next trip to the mountains in America."

"Thank you, Jiro. You're a good friend."

"Come have some hot ramen before you go. There is still time yet."

"I don't know. I should get on the roads before the snow comes."

"You must have a drink with me. Sapporo beer is the best in all of Japan." He pulled Darien toward the small building near the dock. "Come. It will warm you up."

"Okay."

Darien followed Jiro to the quaint wooden house that served as a fishing house, restaurant and bar to the villagers who lived along the icy eastern shore. The moment he stepped inside the warmth and bustle of the quaint building, he felt comfortable and at home. Everyone greeted him with warm cheer, and the old woman who obviously ran the place immediately sat him at their "best" table and brought him a bottle of Sapporo beer as if he'd been expected all along.

After an hour, Darien was surrounded by eight men, young and old, laughing and talking, a few trying out their English and failing miserably, although he'd done no better with his Japanese. The ramen noodles filled him and warmed his insides with their spicy flavoring. And the beer, although bitter, went down quite nicely with the noodles.

Draining the last of his drink, Darien announced to the group that he needed to get on the road. After Jiro translated there was a chorus of disappointed remarks. Bowing and shaking hands, Darien finally made his way to the exit. There the oldest of the group bowed to him and spoke. His Japanese rusty, the only thing Darien clearly heard was the name Koori-Onna.

Darien glanced at Jiro. "What did he say?"

"He said to take great care and do not fall to Koori-Onna's charms. It will be the death of you."

Darien smiled. "Tell him there's no worry of that. Women don't find me all that attractive, not even mythical ice maidens."

Jiro translated to the old man who watched Darien with interest. With a strange smile, he bowed to Darien and opened the exit door for him.

Once Darien was safely buckled into his SUV, the hair stood up on the back of his neck. A shiver raced down his spine. The moment the old man had said her name, a sense of cold dread had crept over Darien.

He knew it was nonsense to be bothered by a myth, a folktale passed down through the generations to give some meaning to tragic events, but he was troubled nonetheless. Maybe it had been the way the old man had looked at him, as if he knew what was to become of Darien, as if he knew some terrible event was in store for him.

Tugging his jacket tighter at the collar, Darien shifted the vehicle in gear and pulled away from the small port, hoping he could beat the snow before it fell.

After an hour on the road, the snow started. But it didn't just fall so much as raged down upon him like a bad omen.

At first big fat flakes floated down, carefree and lazy, but Darien knew that was just the preshow. The dark sky threatened so much more than the pretty flakes of storybook Christmases. After the first fall, the wind picked up and started to howl. At one point it became so fierce, Darien had trouble keeping the SUV on the road.

As visibility reduced close to zero, Darien slowed the vehicle down to ten miles an hour. He prayed silently that there was no one else stupid enough to be out on the roads. Even at this speed, a head-on collision would definitely cause some injuries.

A brutal gust of wind howled against the glass, rattling the vehicle. Darien could feel the cold creeping over his body. Even through the hat, gloves and heavy thermal jacket, the cold still seeped in. He went to turn the dial on the heater but stopped, realizing it was already cranked to the maximum.

He'd been to the coldest places on earth—Antarctica, North Pole, Greenland, but for some reason it felt colder here. Maybe it was the fact that he couldn't get the sense of trepidation out of his system. Something was going to happen.

He shook his head to clear it. "Don't be stupid, man. It's just a silly story."

Even though he said the words, he didn't fully feel the conviction behind them.

When he first heard about the ice maiden myth, he'd done some research on it. Like everything he did, he approached it systematically. But there was no reasoning behind the myth; it was a story and nothing more.

He'd gone on too long without a woman, he thought. He was just lonely. He was pathetic if just the mention of a beautiful woman incited hot dreams. And they'd been extremely hot. He'd woken up a few times, harder than steel.

"Like a damn teenager." He chuckled to himself. He really was pathetic.

No wonder Jessica had left him all those months ago. She had accused him of being too wrapped up in his work, and she'd been right. If he wasn't out in the field researching, he was at home in his office writing about his findings on his laptop, or he was preparing for his next time out in the field.

She hadn't needed him anyway. After a year together, he had realized what a strong independent woman she was. A corporate lawyer, she'd been more interested in getting ahead in her job, owning an amazing wardrobe and hanging with the best people. It still baffled him how they had ever ended up together in the first place. Probably because they had grown up together and their parents had been friends. Other than that, they really hadn't had much in common. Darien certainly hadn't been the right man for her. And she hadn't been the woman for him.

He'd gone too long without a healthy relationship. Maybe when he got to Tokyo he'd go to one of those gentlemen clubs and acquire some female companionship for the night. Something uncomplicated and temporary. Just enough company to break him out of his dry spell.

As he mused over the possibilities, bright lights flashed at him through the windshield. Another vehicle was bearing down at him and at high speed.

Cursing, Darien wrenched the steering wheel. There was no traction on the road. It was pure ice.

He tried to correct the spin he put the vehicle in, but it was too late. He plowed into a huge snowdrift on the side of the road before he could even think.

From the impact, he knocked his head on the steering wheel. Thankfully, the air bag didn't pop. He didn't really want to deal with trying to shove it back into the wheel.

The SUV was still running. Darien put it in Reverse, but it didn't budge. The sound coming from the rear indicated that the tires were spinning in place. There was too much ice.

Cursing again, he banged his fist on the steering wheel, and then shifted it into Park. He was going to have to get out and put something behind the tires to give them some traction.

Pulling his hat down over his ears, Darien opened the door and jumped out into the blizzard. As he made his way around to the back, he searched the surroundings for the other vehicle. There was no way that it didn't also go off the road. Not in this weather, not on this icy stretch of highway. But he couldn't see anything through the howling, blistering white wall of snow.

Opening the hatch on the SUV, he dug through the equipment and found a short-handled shovel, especially designed to dig out of snow and ice. He slammed the hatch shut and proceeded to dig the back tires out of the snow.

After fifteen minutes of digging, Darien climbed back into the SUV and tried to back out. Still the tires spun in place. He got out again and continued to dig, chipping at the ice underneath the heavy blanket of white.

Once more he tried to move the vehicle, to no avail. He was good and stuck. He wasn't going anywhere any time soon, not until the blizzard stopped and he could either flag down someone, or find something to jam under the tires to garner some traction.

Luckily he was well-equipped with thermal blankets, a hot plate, bottled water, dried food and a full gas tank. He could wait it out for at least twelve hours if he had to. He just hoped it didn't come to that.

Darien jumped out into the snow again to go around the back to the hatch. He'd grab some supplies to hunker down for a few hours. As he opened the back, a sound whispered to him on the wind. Shivers, not just from the cold, raced down his spine.

He turned to survey the area. Was there someone there calling to him? Maybe the driver of the other vehicle.

"Darien." The haunting voice echoed all around him. He stared into the blustering snow, desperate to see something, anything concrete.

Something caught his eye, and he turned toward it. A shape materialized in the blinding white.

"Darien, I've been waiting for you."

Darien wiped at his eyes with the back of his gloved hand. Surely he was seeing things. The combination of the blinding snowscape, the fact that his eyes were watering and the Sapporo beer he had downed had to be playing tricks on his vision. Because there couldn't possibly be a woman dressed in a blue kimono floating to him on a wisp of cold air.

The old man's warning sounded in his head. *It will be the death of you.*

"Darien," she whispered on a breeze. Her voice was seductive. A sudden urge to go to her rushed over him. He clamped his eyes shut and fought against the ridiculous notion.

When he opened his eyes again, she was still there, floating above the snow. He noticed she was barefoot, her toenails painted a sensual crimson. With a demure smile she beckoned him to her.

Oh, Darien wanted to go to her, to lose himself in the exquisite beauty of her. But he fought against the urge, knowing full well it was a hallucination brought on by the stories he'd heard and his dire situation. It was just that she seemed so real and not a figment of his overactive imagination.

"It's an illusion," he chanted to himself, then shook his head trying to shake off the haunting image.

"I am no illusion, Darien. I am your destiny."

His foot moved forward. It surprised him. It was as

if he wasn't in control of his body. He knew it was a huge mistake to move into the snowstorm away from the safety of his vehicle, but that didn't stop him from taking another step and another until he was six feet from the bumper of the SUV.

He turned and looked back at the vehicle, stunned that he had moved so far without fully realizing it. He was on autopilot and fueled by the allure of the ice maiden beckoning him to move even farther into the blizzard. Although Darien knew full well that to do so would be his death, he walked even closer toward her.

She smiled at him, and his heart swelled with emotion. She was breathtaking, and he couldn't stop looking at her. Her pale face and perfect painted cupid-bow of a mouth drew him closer and closer until he was so close he knew if he lifted his hand he'd be able to touch the silk of her kimono. But he feared to do just that. Because what if his touch made her disappear? Where would he be then but alone in a violent snowstorm with no hope of survival?

An ache so raw, so violent, pounded in his heart and in his body. He had to touch her; he had to have her, if only for a moment before he died. Because he knew that death was knocking, no, pounding, on his door. And even though he knew that fundamentally, and had no real desire to die, Darien welcomed it.

He reached for her. "Please," he begged. Although he had no idea what he was pleading for. Her touch? Her kiss? Release from this mortal coil? At this point, anything would be a relief to the pain hammering inside him.

Still smiling, she floated down to him. He gasped when at last her hand caressed his cheek. Her touch was like ice, but he didn't shudder from it, not from the cold of it. It felt like heaven on his skin and a shiver of pleasure rushed down his spine.

When she stood next to him, he realized how petite she was. The top of her head came to his chin, and he wanted to envelop her in his arms and hold her until the summer sun came. Instead, he leaned down to her mouth, eager for her kiss.

With her head tilted up, her lips parted in anticipation, it was all Darien could do to stop from putting his mouth to hers, to take her finally. As she met his gaze, she brushed her lips against his and he was done. Nothing now or ever again could feel as good as the cool press of her frozen lips.

Greedily, he drank her in. Wrapping his arms around her, he deepened the kiss. That was when he felt the air being sucked from his lungs. But he didn't care. She was his at long last and that was all that mattered.

With his last breath, he whispered against her lips, *"I'm yours, forever."*

Chapter 2

Although his eyelids were hot, sore and difficult to open, Darien finally forced them apart and looked around. His whole body ached and every move, however small it seemed, caused him blistering agony.

He stared up at the white ceiling and tried to focus on where he was and what had happened. The last thing he could clearly remember was getting stuck in a snowbank on the side of the road to Kushiro. After that, everything was hazy and confusing.

Lifting his head, he gazed down at himself. He was on a platform bed, hard and uncomfortable beneath his back, under a few layers of mocha-colored silk, in a large white room. Except the walls weren't painted, at least with any paint he'd ever seen. They appeared shiny and wet like melting icicles.

There seemed to be no windows in the room, but there was light radiating from somewhere. Not from lamps or any visible light fixtures but almost as if the walls, floor and ceiling glowed from within.

Shifting his position on the bed, Darien lifted up the cover and saw that he was naked. Where were his clothes? Craning his neck, he glanced around the odd room searching for anything familiar, anything to indicate to him that he wasn't going mad. Stacked in one corner appeared to be all the equipment from his SUV. Folded neatly on a chair—also white and glistening like the walls—were his clothes.

He was hoping that it would help to see his things, but it didn't. He was more confused than before. If this was a dream would he really see concrete items like a hot plate and a jerry can of gasoline? Why not dancing naked women with insatiable libidos? That would be way more interesting.

Maybe he wasn't dreaming or hallucinating, but was dead. And this was his purgatory—a pristine white room made out of ice.

Lowering his hands, he ran his fingers over the "mattress" underneath him. The angular lines were smooth and slick to the touch. Curious, he rolled over and looked down the side of his bed. It was completely crafted from ice. The frame, intricately carved with sleek designs, was like crystal and cool to the touch. It seemed impossible, but there it was, and he was lying on top of it. The interesting thing was he wasn't cold. In fact, he didn't feel any chill whatsoever. Not from the air and not from the structure he was on, yet there was no mistaking that he was completely surrounded by a frozen landscape.

He tried to sit up, determined to find out exactly what was going on and where he was, but nausea swept over him, and he had to lay back down to catch his breath. His head ached fiercely, and then he remembered hitting it on the steering wheel when he ran into the snowbank.

As he gathered himself, his thoughts strayed toward the impossible. An image of a breathtaking Japanese woman in a blue kimono filled his mind. He had seen her, hadn't he? She *had* spoken his name.

He pressed his fingers to his lips. They were cool but dry against his skin. The sensation triggered another thought and image. She had kissed him. As sure as he existed, so had she. He could still feel the tingling of ice on his face from her touch.

He wasn't going mad, was he? He'd always been sane and rational. Even as a child he'd analyzed everything, including the possibility of there being a closet monster and if Santa Claus could truly exist. He had always been the levelheaded one, the guy others relied on to explain and reason.

But now, he wasn't too confident. He was completely out of his element, and he hated the lost feeling coming over him.

The sound of a door opening drew his attention to the

far corner of the room. Framed in the doorway stood the woman from his dreams, from his vision of a beautiful woman in a sapphire-blue kimono floating to him across the snow. The woman from the myth.

The ice maiden.

Without meeting his gaze, she entered the room and crossed the floor to his bed. She carried a tray in her arms. On it he could see steam rising from a cup and from a plate. The smell of food wafted to his nose and he inhaled deeply, his stomach growling in response.

Avidly, he watched her as she busied herself next to the bed, setting the tray down on a table. She didn't look at him as she worked. She acted as if he wasn't even there.

"Where am I?" he asked, his voice cracking from thirst.

She avoided his question and handed him the cup, making sure he took it with two hands.

"Where am I?" he asked again, this time in Japanese. Still she didn't answer.

Resigned to her silence, he raised his head and took a sip of the hot liquid. It was some sort of tea and it warmed him instantly, soothing his dry mouth and throat.

He handed it back to her and she set it onto the tray. "Who are you?"

Instead of answering, she spooned up what looked like soup and set it against his lips. He opened his mouth and she fed him. Spoonful after spoonful, she ladled the soup into his mouth until the bowl was empty and his stomach was blissfully full.

Fatigue washed over him and he tried to fight back a yawn, but it was no use. His eyelids drooped, and he wanted nothing but to sleep. He fought it, wanting, needing, answers instead.

"Why won't you answer me?" he demanded. "Where am I? I deserve an answer."

She looked at him then. It was brief but he saw something there in her gaze. Sympathy maybe? Regret?

Before he could ponder it further, she gathered the tray in her arms and started for the door.

"Wait! Please tell me something. Anything."

But she didn't. Without a word, or a second glance, she went through the door and closed it firmly behind her. He was alone again.

Another rush of fatigue surged over him, and he struggled to keep his eyes open. Biting down on his tongue he tried to stay awake. But it was no use. The pull of sleep lulled him under. Slowly, slowly he slipped into the black folds and dreamed of dancing snowflakes in blue.

Chapter 3

He was floating on an iceberg in the middle of the ice sea shelf off the coast of Hokkaido. The strange thing about that was his nakedness.

But he wasn't cold.

He actually felt right at home, standing on the floating ice, gazing out across the vast ocean. He'd always been at home in the cold. There was nothing he liked more than to go snowshoeing after a fresh snowfall or go spelunking in British Columbia at the Columbia Icefield. He'd been born in a winter month and had always felt at home in its grasp.

This wasn't home, though. This was odd and strange and definitely not real.

A dream maybe. A wild, strange dream. Like the ones he'd been having lately since coming to Japan.

Before Darien could figure out what was happening, another iceberg floated up next to his. On it stood a beautiful Japanese woman in a blue kimono. She was exquisite, and he couldn't take his eyes off her.

It was her, the ice maiden from the myth. It was Koori-Onna.

She smiled at him, and he felt every bone in his body melt at the sight. She was stunning. Like the first snowflake of the winter season, perfect in its construction and unique. Every snowflake was an original.

Like her.

When she looked upon him, he became very aware of his state of undress. Her gaze was heated, and he reacted like any hot-blooded male would.

He hardened instantly, his heart fluttering and stomach clenching at the possibility of being with her. If only they weren't floating on icebergs in the middle of the frigid ocean. Why couldn't they have been floating on soft, cushiony beds?

Stranger things had happened—especially in his dreams of late.

As she floated toward him, she slowly undid her kimono and let it slide off her body. She was perfect underneath. High small breasts, the tips painted a delicate rose color, flat belly and a soft flare of hips. The light sprinkling of hair between her thighs was as dark as the mass of shiny ebony hair on her head. Her skin was as pale as moonlight and looked as soft as cream-colored silk.

She raised her hand toward him. "Darien. Come to me. I am yours."

He didn't hesitate. With one giant step, he crossed the threshold separating them. The iceberg didn't even wobble as he stepped onto it. Without a word, Darien gathered her into his arms.

She fit perfectly against his chest, the top of her head touching the bottom of his chin. She smelled like rain and cool winter breezes. Burying his face into her hair, he inhaled her scent, reveling in her.

She reached down between them and grasped his cock in the slim, silky palm of her hand. Darien groaned loudly and ground his teeth as she stroked the length of him. It was all he could do to keep on his feet as she caressed him up and down, up and down. He didn't know it was possible, but he hardened even more. It was almost painful.

She continued to stroke him until he thought he'd go insane. Burying his hands in the silk of her hair, he crushed his mouth to hers, sweeping his tongue between her lips to taste her. She was as cool as mint.

He wanted her. He ached for her. Nothing in his life had ever made him feel this wanton, this lusty. It raged inside him like a caged beast. And he desperately wanted to unleash it. Onto her, into her.

Running his hands down her back, he gripped her around her buttocks and picked her up, to brace her against the icy wall of the berg. He couldn't wait any longer. He had to have her. Without ceremony, he parted her legs with his knee and entered her with one swift thrust.

She cried out and dug her nails into his back.

Koori sat up in bed. Sweat actually dotted her upper lip and the back of her neck. She hadn't experienced that sensation in more years than she could count. She swung her legs around the bed and stood.

Her sleep was ruined now. There was no way she could go back. The dream had been powerful, and vivid. She shivered, remembering the feel of his wide, hard hands on her body. Even now, there was a throb between her thighs.

She was surprised to feel it. Desire was not something she felt often. Or at least not in the last millennia.

Standing, she slipped on her kimono and left her bedroom. She walked to the frozen fireplace and poured from the pot of green tea sitting on the mantel as it was every time she woke, likely deposited there by an unseen servant while she slept.

As she sipped from the cup, she gazed across the expanse of her chamber. It would've been beautiful if it hadn't been her prison for so long. Now she didn't see beauty, only shackles.

While she drank, relaxing her body, she thought of the golden-haired man she'd brought to her home. Maybe it had been a bad idea to do so. She didn't want or need the dreams he'd been inducing. She'd gone on long enough without conflicted emotions that having them now was only a lesson in futility.

Maybe she should go to him now and just end it. She could dispose of him while he slept and he'd never be aware of it. Theoretically he should be dead anyway. That had been her mission when the phantom door had opened to her and she had been compelled to walk to the road. Her goal had been simple. To ferry him from this world to the next. To give him the kiss of death.

But something had stayed her. It might've been the look in his eyes or the words that he had uttered. Words she hadn't ever heard before, and he had whispered them to her as if he had truly meant them.

No. She shook her head. He was more trouble than he was worth. She should end it now before it became worse. Before the magic of this place lashed out at her and punished her even more for what she'd done.

She'd had enough of the punishments. She didn't think she could endure them any longer.

Setting her tea down on the table, she decided she'd go to the room she'd put the sleeping man in and end it. Nothing good could come of it. She'd been a fool to spare his life and bring him here.

What could he possibly do for her? Nothing. He wasn't going to be her savior. There was no such thing. At least not for her.

Chapter 4

Koori watched him sleep from the edge of the bed. Darien, the light-skinned man that had come out of the snow and spoken to her. At first she had come to his room to send him to the next world. But again her hand was stayed. She couldn't do it. Now that he was here in her care, she couldn't ferry him on.

Now she was back in his room watching him. For the last two days and nights, he had slipped in and out of consciousness, babbling on about a snowstorm and a woman in blue.

She assumed he was talking about her.

Groaning, he shifted on the bed, his face grimacing as if in pain. She moved alongside the bed. Hand shaking, she touched his rugged cheek. His skin was hot, slick with sweat. She moved her fingers over him up to his forehead which was also warm and moist. He was definitely fighting a fever.

"*Mizu*," she called out.

Within seconds, a servant woman made entirely out of ice shuffled into the room carrying a medium-sized crystal bowl full of water. The servant handed it to Koori then shuffled back out of the room from where she had come from.

A cloth floated in the water. Koori wrung it out and set it on Darien's forehead. He moaned as she pressed it against his skin. She watched his mouth as he mumbled. He had sensual lips, full and soft.

When she had kissed him, it had been pleasant. For the first time in so long, she had enjoyed the ceremony of giving the kiss of death.

Why she had spared this particular man's life, she still didn't know. It was a puzzle to her and one she hoped to figure out soon.

I'm yours, forever.

His words still haunted her thoughts. Not one of the plethora of men and women she'd encountered over the years had ever come to her willingly. He had been the first.

By having him here in her home—prison really—she was breaking the laws of the curse that had been laid on her. She just hoped he was worth the risk she was taking.

When he groaned again, she dipped the cloth in the water, wrung it out, then rubbed it over his cheeks and down to his neck. Water dripped down and wet the ends of the tawny-colored hair that curled around his ears. She liked the golden color of his hair, the way it almost glowed in the light. Feeling brave, she ran her fingers through his soft waves, reveling in the feel of it on her skin.

He responded to her touch. The corners of his mouth twitched up. Not only did the reaction surprise her, but it pleased her as well. A warmth she hadn't felt in a thousand years started to swell in her belly. She'd almost forgotten what that feeling was.

Wanting that sensation to grow, she continued to wet the cloth and run it over his face and neck. Each time, he moaned or moved his head with her touch. And soon her hesitant touches turned to gentle caresses, with pleasure in mind more than healing.

As he continued to move and flinch, the silk blanket on top of him shifted. Each time more of his chest showed. Koori couldn't help her gaze from drifting down to his body. He was a tall man with wide shoulders, solidly built and appealing to her eyes.

She couldn't remember the last time a man of his coloring or stature had stumbled into her snowstorm. Maybe never. He intrigued her on so many levels; it was a muddled mess in her mind.

Guilt at admiring him as he lay unconscious pulled her gaze away and back to the business at hand. She was here to heal him, help his fever dissipate. It was just that his reaction to her touches seemed like those of a man in the thrall of pleasure.

Setting the cool, wet cloth on his forehead, Koori found she couldn't control her curiosity any longer. Slowly she slid the blanket down, revealing more of him.

She knew he was naked, as she had been the one to remove his wet clothing, but at the time she had only thoughts of his survival on her mind. But now, rare carnal notions swam unhindered in her head.

Licking her lips, she raked her gaze over him, taking in every angle and slope of his well-defined form. He was a man made for the rugged outdoors. His strong but lean arms and trim waist told her he was athletic, maybe a runner, or a hiker—if she remembered his muscular legs correctly. And she had to admit, she did remember the powerful length of them as she had removed his pants.

As Koori took in his beautiful features, she found she itched to touch him. The tips of her fingers actually tingled in anticipation of the hot smoothness of his flesh. Uncertain of how her body would react, she drew a finger down his body, tracing the line between his chest muscles.

The warmth at her center grew, swirling lower to between her legs. The sensation surprised her as she hadn't experienced that kind of pleasure in more years than she wanted to think about. It had been torture to be alone for so long. Once she was a very sensual being, a woman who enjoyed the sexual arts, who excelled at them. It had been so long, she'd forgotten who that woman truly was.

But now, touching this man, the ice solidifying her insides started to melt. Maybe with him she'd finally have a chance to be free of her cold constraints.

Closing her eyes, she settled her hand over his chest. Under her palm she felt the thump of his heart and the heat of his blood rushing through his veins. It'd been so long since she heard that sound, so long since she experienced the rush of life-giving essence that the power of the sensation surprised her.

She moved her hand over him, feeling his flesh, his heat, reveling in his mortal qualities. Oh, what she'd give to be like that again. To have the sensation of touch, and pleasure at her beck and call. To be a real woman again with a man at her side. A man eager to please her, eager to do whatever she wanted him to. Oh, how she longed to have that delight.

Her guilt long gone, Koori let her hand travel lower still. Eyes open wide, she watched as her fingers traced a circle around his navel. She played one tip through the light sprinkling of tawny hair that dipped even lower under the blanket. She knew where it led and for the first time in a millennia, she hungered for it. To feel the hard length of a man in her hand would be her greatest pleasure.

Darien let out a sensual moan as if he was privy to her erotic thoughts. The sound lifted her gaze and she brought it back to his face.

His eyes were open and watching her.

Startled, she snatched her hand back. She dropped her gaze and busied herself with the bowl of water. Embarrassment surged over her, and she wanted to dig a hole in the ice and climb in. Instead, she took up the bowl and started for the door.

Darien reached for her, grasping her wrist. "Wait," he croaked, his voice barely audible. "Don't go."

"You must rest." She pulled from his grip. He was too

weak to offer any resistance. Head down, she continued toward the door.

"Please."

His plea nearly stopped her, but she knew she had to go. She'd been a fool to do what she did. And she'd been caught at it.

When she reached the threshold and turned to close the door, she noticed that he had fallen back asleep. It was for the best, because if she had turned and he'd been watching her, with his vivid blue eyes beckoning her, she was uncertain she'd have been able to leave.

Chapter 5

A stiffness in his neck brought Darien out of a restless sleep. He'd been dreaming of pale eyes in a blinding snow. He'd been dreaming of her, the ice maiden, again.

In one feverish dream, he swore she'd touched him. And not a slight brushing of fingers but a sensual caress full of passion. The image had been so real in his mind that even now he ached in remembrance.

Lifting his arms over his head, he stretched. His body felt better, not as sore and stiff. He wondered how long he'd been in and out of consciousness. A day? Two? A week?

He ran his hand over his chin. His usual five o'clock shadow was now a good half-inch scruff. By the feel of it, he imagined he looked like a crazed mountain man, with his longish scraggly hair and full unkempt beard. He'd just about kill for a shave right now.

After stretching again, Darien sat up. Nausea didn't plague him this time, and he was able to swing his legs over the mattress, and his feet to the floor. Surprisingly, the ice floor wasn't cold.

He stood up and surveyed the room, keeping his eye on the closed door. He really didn't want to be in the buff if he suddenly received company. Although if the ice maiden chose to return at that moment, he wasn't too sure he'd be too put out by it. There was no denying that she was unearthly beautiful and his groin twitched when he thought about her.

An image of them locked in an embrace, her lips traveling his chin and down his neck made his groin twitch even more. Had he dreamed that?

He ambled to the corner where his stuff had been placed. His right leg was still a little achy and he massaged the thigh as he moved. He dressed quickly, and then took stock of the equipment piled high. Everything was there, intact, no obvious damage to any of it.

After he surveyed his items, he put his attention to the walls around him. He placed his hand on the sparkling crystal and rubbed it up and down. It was definitely crafted from ice. It amazed him that something like this could exist. A room, possibly a whole house, constructed from frozen water. Although, there were a few ice bars in Hokkaido; Japan's northernmost island was famous for them. As were other countries including Norway and Sweden, even Canada. So, Darien assumed it was possible. But it just seemed so surreal. Especially since everything in the room had been created from it: the chairs, the bed, the gorgeous four-tier chandelier hanging from the high ceiling that shed no light. All seemingly impossible but all as real as he was.

Or maybe that was the issue. Maybe he wasn't real anymore. He still hadn't resigned himself to actually being awake and aware. There was still the remote possibility that he was in a coma and dreaming all of it.

Curious to see more, he ventured toward the door, opened it and peered out into another large area, also made of ice. This room seemed like a lofty sitting room or parlor, and images of old English castles came to his mind. That's what it all seemed like to him as he turned, eyeing the surroundings—a huge elegant palace made of ice. So instead of the ice maiden, maybe she was the ice princess.

And was he to be the prince charming coming to rescue her? He laughed at that. If Darien was a prince then he was surely dreaming. Besides that, he realized that he had been the one in need of rescuing. If that was indeed what she had done—saved him from freezing to death in the blizzard.

But then all the stories told about her would be untrue, the myth of Koori-Onna a false one. Or this was something else altogether. Maybe he was here for a completely different reason.

Darien continued his search of the palace, becoming more and more intrigued with every ice furnishing he came across. Chairs, tables, the mantel over an unlit fireplace, everything crystalline and glowing pale blue from the inside. It was breathtaking but eerie. And a whisper of dread crept over him. It was too pristine and perfect as if it was constructed all in the hopes of being torn down. As if a well-placed hammer could shatter it into a million tiny crystal shards.

Darien marveled at everything as he walked through rooms and down halls. One thing he did notice was that none of the rooms had windows or doors that led to anywhere but more rooms. The three doors he'd come upon he had opened in hopes of finding a way out, only to find another room to explore.

He didn't know how long he'd moved through the palace. It seemed like hours, because when he happened upon the last room his legs were shaky, but it might've been because of what he found.

This room was different.

It wasn't as large as the others and had lower ceilings. In the middle of the room was a pool of water, a hot springs. Steam rose from the water, filling the area.

Then he saw the ice princess soaking in the water, naked. The steam wasn't so thick that he couldn't fully see her beautiful curves and perfect pale skin.

Her eyes widened when she saw him, and her arms instinctively wrapped around her body, covering her naked breasts.

Hand out toward her, he approached the pool, cautiously. "Don't be afraid."

She watched him curiously but said nothing. By the look in her eyes, he didn't think she was all that indifferent to him coming across her.

"Do you understand English?"

She nodded.

"I want to thank you for saving me." He rubbed a hand over his chin. "At least that's what I think you did," he mumbled as an afterthought. He looked at her, waiting for a response to anything he'd said. She just watched him with those impossibly pale eyes.

He gestured to the pool, hoping to find common ground with her. He was completely out of his element here. How did a man talk to an ice princess supposedly from a thousand-year-old myth? "The water looks inviting. May I join you?"

She didn't answer him, but he thought he saw something change on her face. She didn't look so cold, so unapproachable. Was there an invitation in the slight twitch of her lips?

Slowly, he slipped his boots off and stuffed his socks inside the opening. Hooking his thumbs into the hem of his long-sleeved henley, he pulled it up and over his head. He set it next to his boots, and then proceeded to remove his khaki pants. He shed them quickly, to not frighten her or, he had to admit, embarrass himself. He left his shorts on.

There was something unsettling about having a woman just watching as he undressed, without a word or movement. As if she was studying him objectively and not looking at him as a seminaked man.

As swiftly as he could without slipping and cracking his head open on the icy floor, Darien lowered himself into the scalding hot water. Instantly he relaxed. The heat from the pool massaged and caressed his sore, tired muscles. When he entered he made sure he was on the opposite end as she was. He didn't want to scare her away. Now that they were here together, he wanted to talk to her, wanted to hear her voice. He wanted to know what was going on.

He wasn't usually one to crave human interaction. He could go months out in the bush with no company but nature itself and the few critters that usually found their way into his tent. But he craved it now.

As he sank down into the healing liquid, he found a ledge to sit on. He kept his gaze on her. Only when he was fully submerged did she seem to relax, unfurling her arms and sinking back into the water. She kept his gaze the entire time.

He felt both unnerved and aroused as she watched him. Her actions dictated that he stay away, but at the same time, he got the strong sensation that she wanted him to breech the space between them. She was definitely the most confusing woman he'd ever been around. He supposed considering the circumstances of his situation that probably wasn't saying too much.

"You know, this is all very strange. I'm in a palace made of ice with a woman who I believe is named Koori-Onna."

She flinched a little at her name. He wondered how long it'd been since she heard it spoken out loud by someone. He had a feeling that she didn't have too many visitors in her frozen home.

"You are Koori-Onna, aren't you?"

She nodded.

"Am I dead? Did you freeze my insides like the stories say?"

"Do you feel frozen?"

The sultry sound of her accented voice startled him. Despite the heat from the water, gooseflesh rose on his skin. The sensation tightened all the muscles in his thighs and other lower regions.

"No," he finally answered after the shock of hearing her speak wore off.

"Then you are not."

He took the start of their conversation as an opening to move closer to her. He could've been completely off base, but he knew if she truly didn't want to be around him, she would've gotten out of the water the moment he entered the pool.

"Why am I here? Why didn't you kill me as the legend says?"

She stared at him for a few seconds, under the hood of her long black eyelashes, then shook her head. "I don't know."

She looked sad as she spoke and Darien had the sudden urge to cross the pool in one swift motion and gather her in his arms. For the first time since he'd seen her, vulnerability shone through her stoic exterior. He imagined it was something she usually didn't reveal to anyone.

Why him? What was the reason he was here and not lying dead in some snowstorm?

He shook his head, the truth or nontruth of the situation was making his head spin. "I just can't believe this. How can this be real? How can you be real?"

"You are a scientist, yes?"

He nodded.

"Then can you not see and touch what is around you?"

"Yes."

"Do you doubt your own observations?"

She was right. He did doubt. "Yes."

"Why?"

"Because this can't possibly be real. It's a myth. You are a myth, a story passed down from generation to generation over a thousand years."

"I am real, Darien. As real as you are."

"How do you know who I am?"

Her lips curled up then, in a shy smile. "I don't know exactly. Just as you have heard stories of me, maybe I have heard stories of you."

He smiled in return, his gaze not leaving her face. She was spectacular to watch. So dainty and elegant, like a porcelain doll.

"Your English is very good."

"I've had a long time to learn."

He wondered what her skin would feel like if he touched her. Would she be cold to the touch? Or would he feel the warmth inside her?

Her smile faded as if she were privy to his thoughts. Maybe she could read his mind. Maybe that was how she knew who he was. He really hoped that wasn't the case, especially with the way he'd been imaging her.

Naked, wrapped around his body, kissing his face and other parts of him.

She shifted in the water and Darien knew she was getting ready to escape.

Before she could get out of the water, Darien crossed the pool. "Please don't go." He reached out and grasped her arm. Despite the heat from the water, her flesh was still icy cold, but he didn't let go.

She looked down at his hand on her arm then back up to his face. He saw confusion there, but also longing. God, she was desirable. He'd never wanted a woman as much as he wanted her right now. Every part of his body ached for her.

When her lips parted, Darien leaned into her, eager to have her mouth. Her eyes widened as he moved in, but she made no attempt to pull away. She stayed very still, stiff under his touch, as his lips brushed hers.

It was then that the room shook.

Chapter 6

The whole room moved as if something had picked it up and rattled it. Panicked, Koori tried to scramble out of the pool, but the motion of the ground slapped her firmly into Darien's lap. He wrapped his arms around her as the walls in the room started to crack.

The breaking sound filled the room. It was so loud she wanted to put her hands over her ears and squeeze her eyes shut. She'd never heard such a noise before, especially not in her home.

She didn't know what was happening, but it almost felt like an earthquake. It was improbable, but not impossible. She remembered the last two powerful quakes to hit Japan. One in 1923 and the last in 1995, but both had occurred on the main island and hadn't affected

Hokkaido all that much. Maybe it was just the northern island's turn to be blasted.

Koori clutched Darien as pieces of ice fell from the walls, shattering into tiny shards on the hard floor. She couldn't believe the walls were breaking. She didn't think it would ever be possible.

She should know; she'd tried breaking them apart herself on many occasions.

During her first year imprisoned in the ice palace, she'd lifted every piece of furniture she could and beat against the walls. All that ever came of it was broken furniture, which was magically reconstructed the next day. Every five years or so after that, she tried again, but to no avail. Everything she had tried to use to break the ice had failed.

Until now. But this was not of her making.

Then she glanced at Darien who was hugging her close and eyeing the shaking room, and she wondered. Could this be the reason she was compelled to bring him here? Could he be the catalyst to the changes happening right now?

Finally the room stopped vibrating. One last piece of ice dropped from the far wall onto the ground and slid across the floor to fall into the hot pool. Steam hissed the second it hit the water. Slowly it dissolved into nothing.

They both watched it in silence.

Suddenly conscious of Darien's arms around her and the heat from his body, Koori pushed out of his embrace and scrambled out of the pool.

"Wait!" he called.

She couldn't. It was all too much for her to handle. She grabbed her kimono from the floor, slid it on and raced from the room before Darien could get out of the water and touch her again.

She sprinted down the hallway toward the east wing and her private chambers. She passed two of her servants standing to attention along the way, but they paid her no mind. Their only purpose was to see to her physical needs. Her mental needs were her own.

When she reached the double doors to her rooms, she pushed them open without pause and shut them firmly behind her. In her mind she summoned two guards to stand at her doors. She didn't want Darien to stumble upon her if he haphazardly searched the castle for her. She needed time alone to gather her thoughts, which seemed ironic to her since she'd been alone for so long. She'd wished countless times for someone to talk to, someone that she could touch and be touched by, and all her wishing had brought Darien to her.

Yet here she was squirreled away in her room, knees trembling, too afraid to let him get close to her. Or was it the fear of what might happen if she did that made her shudder?

Koori walked into her sitting room and poured herself a cup of warm sake that was waiting for her on the small table. She drank it quickly, and then poured another. She sat, then, pretending there was a roaring fire in the frozen hearth.

For a thousand years she'd been cursed to live in this ice palace. The only times she'd been allowed out were to bring death to those stranded in snowstorms. It was her penance for a crime she committed over a hundred lifetimes ago.

During the first decade, Koori spent it grieving for the man who she had lost—her lover, Shiro Tagawa, and for the man whom she'd wronged—her husband, Kyoshi Iwasaki. Her affair had doomed them all and had sent her to this hell to spend an eternity.

Her husband had died in a snowstorm after discovering her and Shiro together. In his anger and dismay, he ventured into a blizzard no man could survive. She often wondered if he had done it deliberately to kill himself. She hadn't ever thought that Kyoshi loved her enough to do such a thing. Love had never been part of their marriage.

Arranged when she was just fourteen, Koori had married the powerful daimyo of the land she was born to. He had not been a kind or gentle man. She lost her virginity violently the night of her wedding and every coupling with Kyoshi after that night had been steeped in brutality.

It wasn't until she'd met a young foolhardy artist named Shiro did she finally understand the meaning of making love. She knew it was wrong, but she'd gone on so long without kindness and gentleness that Shiro's alluring face and laugh couldn't sway her from her desires.

They both had paid for it with their lives.

After Kyoshi's body was found frozen a mere mile from the house, his brother, Junzo, a man rumored to possess powerful magic, came to find Koori and Shiro.

Shiro was brutally executed in front of her. Even after so long, she could still see the macabre scene in her dreams. With Koori, he wanted her to suffer. He had called her an ice-hearted whore and murderess. Instead of killing her outright, he put a curse on her.

To ferry those stranded in the snow to their icy death until she found someone that could love her for who she truly was. Only then would she be free of her icy prison. How could anyone love their murderer?

She tossed back the rest of her sake and stared into the empty cup. Maybe Darien was her one and only chance at redemption.

But she was scared. Hope could be such a damaging thing.

Chapter 7

After getting out of the pool and meagerly drying off, Darien searched the castle for her. He had to know what was going on. She couldn't leave him without answers. The earthquake was just the final straw in an already heavy load on his mind.

He assumed she probably had a private wing of her own. Or it could be that he'd read too many fairy tales as a child and thought that all princesses had rooms of their own in the castle. But he had nothing else to go on, so that was the best he could come up with.

After an hour of blindly walking down hallway after hallway, he finally came across a new area that looked different. Two huge guards made of ice were standing in front of a set of double doors.

When he approached, the guards came alive. Both had been sculpted wearing matching uniforms and with long pointy spears in their massive ham-sized hands. They both aimed the spears at him as he took another step forward.

"Koori!" he shouted.

No answer.

He tried again. "Koori! We need to talk. I have to know what's going on."

Several seconds ticked by before, finally, the guards stood down, lowered their spears and stepped off to the side of the doors. Cautiously, Darien moved forward and gripped the handle to one door. Eyeing both guards, looking for any sign that they would attack, he slowly opened the door and slid through.

Koori sat on a golden silk-covered chaise waiting for him, her back straight and her hands resting demurely in her lap.

"Okay, what the hell was that?"

"You mean my guards?"

"No—" he shook his head "—well, yes, they're definitely strange, but I mean the earthquake in the hot springs."

"I don't know."

"Does it happen often?"

"That was the first time."

Darien ran a hand through his hair as he paced the room. "Why did it happen?"

She shook her head but didn't meet his gaze.

He stopped in front of her. "You're not telling me the truth."

She looked at him then, and he saw a commanding spark in her eye. "I'm not a liar. I just don't know what is going on."

"Start from the beginning then." He sat down beside her. "How did you get here?"

She smoothed a hand down her kimono as she spoke. Was it nerves or guilt he saw in her face?

"Many years ago, I committed a terrible act and betrayed my vow and this is my penance. I am forced to live in this place like a prisoner. The only time I am allowed to leave is to ferry those lost in the snow to their deaths." She wouldn't look at him as she told her story. He couldn't blame her; it wasn't pleasant to hear.

"But you saved me and brought me here."

She nodded. "There was something different about you. Some quality that even now I can't name. You were the first person who ever willingly came to me." She licked her lips nervously. "And you looked at me. Really looked." She raised her head and met his gaze.

Her eyes should've startled him. They were so pale, so luminous, and completely unnatural, but they drew him in like a moth to a flame. Her gaze enchanted him in a single moment and he was lost to her.

Had it been magic that compelled him to her in that snowstorm? Did she cast some spell over him? If she did, she seemed utterly ignorant of it. He couldn't say why he had been drawn to her. There wasn't just one certain thing, not one quality that mesmerized him. It was everything about her. Her cold beauty stunned him, but she had an inner warmth he sensed deep inside her that made him want to touch her, to be with her.

If it was magic then he was bewitched and there was nothing he could do about it. Or *wanted* to do about it.

Hesitantly, he caressed her cheek. Her skin was soft like creamed silk. He once touched a petal of a dewy flower during the early days of spring and thought it the softest thing he'd ever touched, but it didn't compare to the reality of her.

"You're the most beautiful woman I've ever seen."

She gave him a small smile and leaned into his touch. He stroked her cheek and ran the pad of his thumb over her plump, pink mouth. Her lips parted on a sigh. He took that as an invitation for more.

Leaning in, he tilted her head up and lightly brushed his lips against hers. He was hesitant at first, testing the waters. When she didn't draw back, Darien deepened the kiss, the tip of his tongue dipping inside her mouth.

She tasted of icy cold mint. Happy memories of all the times he'd spent skiing in the mountains flooded back to him. He loved the winter and everything it brought. The first snowfall, icicles hanging from the eaves of his family home, brisk breezes, the sense of belonging especially during the holidays. It all came to him in that single moment of kissing her.

She tasted of his home back in Montana where the winters lasted for five months of the year. And the summers were unusually sultry and pleasant.

He kissed her until he thought the room was shaking beneath him again. But when he broke away and stared into her eyes, he realized it was just him. He was vibrating with desire like an overeager teenage boy on his first date with the girl of his dreams.

Except she *was* the girl of his dreams. At least from the dreams he'd been having for the past five or six nights since arriving in Japan. They were linked somehow. He knew it as fundamentally as he knew the Earth was round and spun on its axis.

Although he was a scientist and everything about this situation screamed that it was impossible, he believed in it. He believed in her.

"I don't know why I'm here, but I'm glad that I am." He brushed a stray dark hair from her brow and leaned in to kiss her again.

This time as he took her mouth, she wrapped her arms around him, burying her hands in his hair. Each small moan that escaped her lips he swallowed down, eager to hear more, willing to give her more to get that sound. He wanted to please her.

His hands at her back, he gathered her closer, while he nibbled on her bottom lip and moved on to her chin. At first she was stiff and her skin cool even through the silk of her kimono, but he could feel the rise in temperature with each gasp from her lips. It was as if she was heating up from his embrace.

While he continued to feast on her neck and the curve of her shoulder, she ran her hands down his back. He could feel the press of her nails, and that sent sparks of pleasure zinging over him. Instantly he was hard, his erection straining against the increasingly tight fit of his pants.

An image from one of his dreams flashed behind his eyes. Koori naked, with her hand wrapped around the hard length of him. He groaned remembering the feel of her cool skin on his hot searing flesh. He bit down lightly on her shoulder urging a moan from her lips.

The sound of the doors slamming open brought both their heads up. Koori screamed when one of the guards marched into the room with his spear pointed at Darien.

Darien jumped to his feet. He really had no intention of getting shish-kebabbed by an eight-foot iceman with an anger problem. He put his hands up to ward off the attack.

"Whoa, man, point that thing somewhere else." To his chagrin the guard kept coming.

Koori stood and marched toward the guard, her hands fisted at her sides. *"Shuushi!"*

The guard slowed but still advanced on them. By this time, Darien was behind the chaise hoping the thick ice would protect him. Except the point on the spear looked like it could pierce ten times the thickness of the sofa.

Koori stood right in front of the advancing iceman with no evidence that she was going to move. *"Shuushi!"* she shouted again.

This time it stopped. It lowered its sword and almost appeared to look sheepishly at her.

"Darien, go back to your room."

"What?"

"Please, return to your room. It won't hurt you if you just leave."

He hesitated. He didn't want to leave her, especially

when he didn't quite know what was going on. Was the ice guard going to hurt her when he was gone?

Koori turned and looked at him. "I will be fine," she said, as if reading his mind again. "It won't hurt me. But you must leave. It will most definitely hurt you."

Seeing the serious look in her eyes, Darien nodded and then went to exit the room.

"I will come to you later. Please don't come looking for me again."

As he passed her and the guard he noticed a few pieces of ice lying on the ground, as if something had just melted. But he couldn't tell if it had come from the guard or from Koori.

Chapter 8

By the time Darien decided to take a break from pacing his room, he swore there was a groove in the floor. But he didn't know what else he could do. It wasn't as if there was a television to watch or a gym he could work out in to pass the time.

For the past day or more, he really couldn't tell, he'd been alone. Koori hadn't come to see him like she said she would. Worry for her made him a bundle of nerves and energy with no outlet.

Between doing sit-ups, push-ups and running the halls, he was going mad with just his paranoia and dread-filled thoughts to keep him company. He'd gone to the hot springs twice, but she hadn't been there. He'd gotten into the water hoping she'd show up. She hadn't.

Despite the guards at her door, he'd gone there twice as well, yelling for her to open the doors. But there was no response. The guards hadn't even moved, except when he got too close to the doors, and then the spears came down. He got pricked in the arm at that point.

When he returned to his room, food and drink had been deposited onto the table. So, at least he wouldn't starve to death. But he felt as if he was starving, and it didn't have anything to do with food.

He ran a hand through his hair and sighed. He had to be losing his mind. There was no other explanation for everything that had happened, everything that he'd seen so far. It was like an episode of *The Twilight Zone* and he was the guest star. He really hoped he didn't get killed off as so many guest stars had in the past.

Darien startled when the door opened.

Koori came in, carrying another tray. This time, there were two plates of steaming hot food. Head down, she walked to the small table, set the tray upon it, and then nervously turned toward him and lifted her gaze.

"Are you hungry?"

Standing, Darien nodded, then came toward her. She sat in one of the chairs and swept her hand toward the other gesturing for him to sit. He did.

"Are you okay? I thought maybe the guards had hurt you."

She gave him a small smile. "I'm perfectly fine as you can see. Please do not worry. The guards would never harm me." She poured the sake into small cups and handed one to him. Then she set a plate of noodles and vegetables in front of him. The scent of the hot food tickled his nose. His stomach growled reminding Darien that he hadn't eaten in a while.

"Please eat," she said.

Darien dug into the noodles with gusto. The second the spicy pasta hit his tongue he forgot that he had so many questions to ask her. Instead, he shoveled the food in, only taking long enough breaks to drink sake.

When he was finished, he set his fork down on the plate and leaned back in his chair, contented. He sighed and rubbed at his chin. "I'm sorry. I didn't realize how hungry I was."

She shook her head. "No, I'm sorry. I should have brought food to you sooner."

"It's all right."

He stared at her across the table. It was the strangest thing sitting in this room of ice, having something as mundane as dinner. An act so simple took on new meaning in this unusual environment. So many questions swirled in his head.

"Where does the food come from? Every time I left the room and came back there was a tray of something on the table."

"All my physical needs are taken care of. I only have to ask for it and one of the servants brings it to me."

"So if you wanted a bottle of beer, you would get it?"

She nodded. "Do you want a beer? I can get it for you."

"No." He shook his head. "I was just using that as an example. How does it work?"

"I don't know exactly. It's like magic, I suppose. The man that imprisoned me here was very powerful."

"Like magic," he murmured while he played his fingers through the scruff on his chin. "It's funny. I was the last person ever to believe in it. But since arriving here—" he chuckled "—I might have to amend my beliefs."

She looked down into her lap as she spoke. "Yes, but unfortunately it isn't all for fun."

"No, I suppose it isn't." He ran a hand over his chin again. "Have you ever tried to leave?"

She glanced at him and he saw a spark of something in her eyes. Anger maybe. "Many times. It is pointless. The only time there is a door to the outside is when I must go to the road. A few times I have tried to veer off the path only to be right back where I started." Her face tightened as she spoke as if just telling the story made her angrier and angrier. "I have tried to break down these walls with everything I could think of, only to have it reform again."

He could see a multitude of emotions cross her face—hope, loss, anger, regret and despair.

"There's no hope that I can leave?"

"If you can find a way out, you may take it."

"So, I'm stuck here then, like you." He hadn't meant for it to sound final, but the reality of his situation just hit him in full force like a sledgehammer to the face. He was never going home again.

"Yes, like me." She stood, tossing her cloth napkin onto the table. "I'm truly sorry for that. But I could not…" Tears welled in her eyes. "I could not kill you like the rest." She turned on her heel and marched for the door.

Darien was up out of his chair in her wake. He reached for her arm and spun her back around. The tears were now falling freely down her pale cheeks to dot her silk kimono.

She tried to pull from his grasp, but he held firm. "I'm sorry. I didn't mean to sound angry or ungrateful. I guess in the back of my mind, I'm still holding on to the hope that this is all a dream and that I'll wake up soon."

"This is no dream, Darien." Her voice quivered. "I know this because I have been trying to wake for over a thousand years."

Darien pulled her close and wrapped his arms around her. At first she resisted him, but he wouldn't relinquish his tight hold on her. He wanted her to know how much he felt for her, how much her situation affected him. Finally, she stopped fighting him. Sighing, she fisted her hands in his shirt and laid her head against his chest.

He ran a hand down her back, and buried his face into her hair. He loved the smell of her. He inhaled deeply. She was so petite in his arms. He had a sudden urge to sweep her up and cradle her in his lap, to keep her safe from everything that would see her harm. She brought out the protector in him. No other woman had ever done that to him.

"I'll find a way out, Koori. I'll find a way for the both of us to leave."

Pulling back, she looked up at him, brow furrowed. "You would want to help me escape?"

He smoothed a hand down her hair. "Yes. I want you to come with me. We can escape together."

"Why? Why would you do this for me? When I have brought you to this place for an eternity?"

He kept her gaze, drowning in the pale pools of her eyes. "Because you don't deserve to stay here any longer. You deserve to have a life outside of these walls. No matter what you did, I think you've paid for it a long time ago."

Another tear rolled down her cheek and Darien caught it on his fingertip. As he brought his finger to his mouth, her lips parted on a gasp. He licked the salty liquid off his tip.

Cupping her cheek with his hand, he tilted her mouth up to meet his. He leaned down and brushed his lips against hers, once, twice until she gasped from it. Swallowing down her whimper, Darien covered her mouth with his and kissed her hard.

She moaned as he took her mouth, sweeping his tongue between her lips. This time she was flavored by spices and sake. Warm and inviting. And he couldn't get enough of the taste of her.

Wrapping a hand behind her neck, Darien bent her back and deepened the kiss. Although he'd just eaten, he felt ravenous for her, as if he'd not eaten or drank in more days than he could count. She was his sustenance, his drink, and only kissing her, having her body next to his, could sate his hunger.

Nibbling on her bottom lip, Darien broke the kiss and proceeded to press his mouth to her chin and neck. Her skin was cool under his touch, but he could feel a slight rise in temperature with each stroke of his lips. Her flesh was warming from his eager touch. And that just incited him further.

Moving his hands down, he swept her into his arms. She gasped at his actions, but as he walked with her to the bed, she wrapped her arms around his neck and held on.

When they neared the bed, Koori reached up and slid the pins out that were holding her hair up. Her mass of ebony hair tumbled down around her, sweeping over her shoulders like a dark curtain of silk. She smiled at him as he set her down onto the bed.

He watched her face as he kneeled down beside her. In her eyes, he saw both trepidation and need. He understood both with equal measure. Being locked up in a prison without human contact for a thousand years had made her freeze up inside, but he hoped that he could help thaw her. He wanted to feel her flesh warm with every caress of his hands, with every touch of his lips.

"I want to look at you, Koori. You are so beautiful."

Licking his lips, Darien untied her kimono and slowly pulled the two halves apart revealing her perfect pale flesh. He had to bite down on his lip to stop himself from pressing his mouth to her taut nipples on her gorgeous breasts. He'd never seen a woman with such flawless skin. He wondered if she'd feel like silk under his fingers.

He trailed his gaze over her, as if his eyes could touch and caress. From the tips of her breasts to the light sprinkling of dark hair at the V of her legs, everything was exquisite.

Darien felt the shivers radiate over her body as he

leaned down and trailed his tongue over her nipples, sucking one between his lips. The moans he pulled from her with each suck of her breasts made him quiver with pent-up desire. It was all he could do not to devour her in one greedy gulp.

He knew he had to go slowly, to show her with each touch, each kiss, just how desirable she was to him, but to do so would take every ounce of restraint he'd ever possessed.

Chapter 9

With each deliberate flick of his tongue, Koori thought she'd go mad with desire. Electrifying blows zigzagged down her torso and gathered deep within her sex. She'd not felt something so powerful, so pleasurable for so long the sensation nearly staggered her. It was as if she were a virgin all over again. But this time, her lover was a gentleman, not a barbarian.

She bowed her back as Darien trailed his tongue to the valley of her breasts and down the line of her torso. He stopped at her navel and nipped playfully at her skin. The whiskers on his chin added a delicious contradiction to the soft press of his lips. She flinched at the tingling sensation between her legs. She knew if he touched her there, she'd be ready for him.

As he brushed his fingertips lightly across her inner thighs, she gasped. He was so close to her, so close she could feel his hot breath on her flesh. Jolts of bliss fired through her. She fisted her hands in the silk cover on the bed in preparation for the orgasm she could already feel building deep inside her. It was going to be hard and explosive.

"You are so damn beautiful, Koori."

"But my skin…it is so cold. How can you stand to touch me?"

He smiled at her then, his eyes wide and dark with desire. "I can feel the heat inside." With one finger, he traced the outline of her navel, and then dipped lower over her pubic mound. In one deft stroke, he separated her slick folds.

Gasping, she arched her back. She'd never been so near orgasm before in such a short time. It was because she'd gone too long without it, without pleasure and passion. During her first years imprisoned, she had only her memories of her past lover, Shiro, to keep her warm.

But now here was this man eager to give her as much as he could.

"You're so hot and wet for me. You're driving me crazy."

Tears brimmed in her eyes. She brought a hand up to wipe them away before Darien could see them there. She didn't need or want his sympathy. Not now. Not ever. She just wanted him.

After pressing an openmouthed kiss to just above her sex, Darien made his way up her body and settled in beside her. She could feel the hard length of him pressing against her leg. He smiled down into her face and lightly traced his finger over her mouth.

"Are you ready for me?"

Too overcome with emotion to form any words, she just nodded. She was more than ready for him. For a thousand years, she'd been waiting for him.

Standing, Darien quickly pulled his shirt off, and then his pants and shorts. He lay back down beside her. Bringing his hand up, he cupped her cheek, then leaned down and kissed her. It was a beautiful, beguiling kiss. A fairy-tale kiss.

Koori moaned into his mouth and trailed her hand down his body. She needed to feel him in her hand. He was hot and heavy against her palm, like silk and steel meshed together. She stroked him once, then twice, until he broke the kiss and gasped.

"I want you bad, Koori," he groaned, "I have to be inside you now."

"Yes," she breathed, "yes, I want that, too. I want you."

Crazy with the need to have him, she rolled him onto his back and lay on top of him. Purring low in her throat, she pressed kisses to his chin and neck. She trailed her tongue over his pulse points and up to the lobe of his ear to suck it into her mouth. All the while she continued to stroke him. "I'm hungry for you, Darien. It's you who I have been waiting for, for so long."

Still gripping him, Koori moved down his body until she was straddling his thighs. Leaning forward, she flicked her tongue over the tip of his hard length. Darien clamped his eyes shut and moaned as she took him into her mouth. She licked and sucked him until she could feel his legs quivering. He was close to climax. To prevent him from coming too soon, she gripped him at the base of his erection and squeezed.

"Koori, I can't hold on," he panted.

She held him still until he softened a little and retained his control. Then she licked down the length of him wanting him to lose it all over again. "Yes, you can."

His eyes were dark and hooded. The muscles ticked along the rugged line of his jaw. She loved that look about him. Dark, fierce, barely holding on. She'd remember that look for the rest of her days.

After one final stroke of her tongue, she moved up his body to straddle his hips. The wait was destroying her. She'd waited long enough to find bliss. She held him firmly in her hand as she lowered herself. Inch by exquisite inch, he filled her. He was a big man, but still the perfect size for her. When she was fully seated, she held herself still and looked at him.

She dreamed of finally being set free. And he'd been sent to her. Darien was her ultimate salvation.

She rubbed her hands up and down his chest, enjoying the way his hard muscles felt under her palms. Watching his face, she contracted the muscles of her sex, squeezing him tight inside her. Every flicker and grimace of emotion that flashed over his handsome face gifted her some of the power she'd lost over the years. She didn't feel so helpless or hopeless any longer. Even if she never escaped these icy walls, Darien had at least given her that back.

As she started to rock her hips, Darien reached up and molded her breasts in his hands. He squeezed and flicked his thumbs over her nipples. Waves of pleasure swept over her and she arched her back to catch them cresting. Up and down, back and forth, she moved on him, finding a rhythm, squeezing her muscles with every stroke.

She watched his beautiful face contort with strain as she quickened her pace. She knew he struggled for control and that he was quickly losing it as she took him up and over. There was a sense of power in that, and she reveled in it.

"I can feel you burning up," he panted. "So damn hot." Darien moved one hand down to where they joined. He circled his fingers into her slick core, finding her pleasure point with expert ease.

He stroked her, as she stroked him. Firmly, pushing her toward climax. Biting down on her lip, she tried to stop from screaming out his name.

Grabbing hold of his shoulders, she picked up her pace, moving faster, harder, taking them to the edge. As the first crest of orgasm mounted inside, she dug her nails into his flesh. With a loud drawn-out moan, she pushed down on him, filling herself completely with his hot male flesh.

He pressed down on her sensitive bundle of nerves one more time and flipped her over that edge. She collapsed forward onto his chest as she spiraled toward her climax. He wrapped his arms around her, burying himself deep, soaring over into ecstasy with her.

He found her mouth and kissed her hard as the delirious passion drowned them. Everything went white behind her eyes and she thought she'd pass out. Everything was clearer, everything brighter in her mind's eye. And she knew deep down inside that everything she'd ever wished for would come true.

Chapter 10

Darien didn't know how long they had lain there on the bed; arms and legs tangled together, the scent of sex still heavy in the air. It could've been a few minutes or two hours, he couldn't tell. Time failed to mean anything anymore. He wasn't even sure how long he'd been in the ice palace.

He thought about what it would mean if he was stuck here in this strange reality for an eternity. Rubbing a lazy thumb down the soft skin of Koori's arm, he considered that it may not be a hardship after all. He wouldn't lack for anything—he had clothing, a bed to sleep in, food would be provided, and he had her. He could think of worse fates to stumble into.

But still he clung to the hope that there was a way

out. There was something different about the icy walls in the past couple of days. They'd changed somehow. He didn't think they were as solid as they once had been. And he knew it had something to do with him.

When Koori stirred beside him, he pulled her up onto his chest. A sigh of contentment escaped his lips.

She nuzzled into him and smiled. "You seem very satisfied."

"Yeah, I guess I am." He rubbed her arm, reveling in the fact that her skin was not nearly as cool as it had been before.

"Good. Because I am, as well. You're very good at sex."

He laughed. "Well, thank you very much. I've been practicing."

That made her laugh.

Darien loved the sound of her throaty chuckle. It provoked a surge of desire to rush over him. Wrapping both hands around her waist, he pulled her up to his mouth. She was still giggling when he covered her lips with his. The laugh was quickly replaced by a long satisfied moan as they kissed.

He nipped and nibbled at her bottom lip, enjoying the little mewls she made each time he did it. Trailing just the tip of his tongue over her lips then into her mouth, he stroked her jawline with the tips of his fingers. He loved kissing her.

And that's when the room started to shake.

Like before, the floor and walls trembled. A sound like thunder echoed through the room. Cracks started to show in the ice.

Koori clutched Darien as the bed rocked back and forth, and not in a good way. The quake seemed to be a hell of a lot more violent than before. Furniture upended and crashed to the floor. Some pieces shattered on impact.

"What's happening?" Koori asked, her voice quivering with fear.

"I don't know. I was just going to ask you that."

Darien didn't quite know, but he was starting to suspect how Koori was attached to the palace, her prison. Each time she touched him or he touched her, the world around them seemed to protest. And now that they'd made love, it was having a temper tantrum. Maybe afraid that its hold on Koori was slowly slipping away.

He couldn't really explain it or understand it in any other way.

"I think the walls are coming down."

She looked at him then, her eyes wide, hope and questions in them. She understood what he was insinuating. Maybe he really was on to something and not wishful thinking.

As the room moved, vibrating and shaking violently, pieces of ice fell from the walls and ceiling. At first they were small pieces, the size of oranges and baseballs, breaking apart and sliding around the floor where they hit.

One small bit cracked Darien in the shoulder. It smarted where it hit. He imagined if it were any bigger it would've definitely left some damage. That was when he saw the enormous crack in the ceiling near the four-tier chandelier.

In seconds, he was off the bed, pulling Koori with him.

She looked around the room in panic, as the walls and ceiling continued to crack and break apart. The noise was deafening, and Darien had to yell over the clamor.

"We need to get somewhere safe. If that ceiling comes down it'll crush us."

He felt odd dashing around the room stark naked, but there really wasn't any time to consider it. If they didn't get out of the room, one or both of them were going to get hurt.

Hand in hand, they ran to the door, dodging the rain of ice chunks. Darien twisted the doorknob and went to yank the door open, but it wouldn't come.

"It's locked."

Koori shook her head. "Impossible. This door has no lock."

He tried it again, turning and pulling on it as hard as he could. Still it wouldn't open. Maybe the shifting walls had inadvertently crushed down on the door. They were stuck in the room without another exit.

Darien turned and examined the room, looking for something they could hide under or near that wouldn't shatter and break. He had visions of the air being filled by flying ice shrapnel as things inside continued to shatter.

A thunderous cracking resonated through the room. He could actually feel the sound waves rolling over his skin. It was difficult to discern where it originated from, but Darien raised his head and looked at the ceiling.

Without a doubt, it was coming down.

Crouching, he pulled Koori to the floor and covered her with his body. He hoped they were close enough to the wall that the ceiling would miss crushing them. He didn't really want to go out this way.

This whole thing was a cruel joke, and he wasn't laughing.

After another thunderous warning, the roof collapsed. A slab twelve feet long and wide fell and crushed the king-sized mattress that they'd been lying on. The bed's frame shattered under the weight of the ice. Shards burst out to the sides like that shrapnel Darien feared and peppered him across his back and legs. Thankfully none pierced his skin, just nicked him like tiny razor blades. Pain seared him from toe to head and he winced to stop from crying out.

And just like that, the room ceased to shake. Sucked into a silent vacuum, it was as if the event had never happened.

Koori blinked up at him. "Is it over?" Her voice was so small and full of fear. He wrapped his arms around her and hugged her close, running a soothing hand over her hair.

"I think so."

Still linked together, they stood and surveyed the damage. Every piece of furniture had been smashed into small pieces. There were small holes in the walls. In one instance, Darien could peer through one and see the next room. The most telling evidence of the quake was the giant gaping hole in the ceiling.

Taking Koori's hand in his, they walked to the center of the room and looked up. Through the jagged hole, they could clearly see something gray and swirling.

Storm clouds, Darien thought. Bitter cold air rushed through the room and Koori nuzzled closer to him. Gooseflesh popped up all over his skin.

Darien had no doubt that it was the sky above him. The palace had been breached. There was a way out.

"This is it, Koori, our way out."

"What?"

He nodded toward the gaping hole. "We can climb up and go through that to the outside."

"How?"

"I have rope, grappling hooks, everything we need." He glanced toward the corner where Koori had stacked all of his equipment from the ditched SUV. It was lucky that she had possessed the presence of mind to bring his things with him. Or maybe it was fate.

He was never one to believe in such things, more confident to rely only on what he could see, touch and measure. But with the way events were turning out, he couldn't rely on stone-cold logic anymore—because everything that had happened since waking on the bed of ice just didn't exist within that logical realm.

She shook her head. "It won't let us leave."

He held her by the shoulders and looked into her eyes. "We have to try, Koori. It's our only opportunity."

When she met his gaze, he saw a kaleidoscope of emotions in the pale depths. He could imagine what she was feeling—fear and hope. He felt it, too. Hope that they could be free of the ice prison and fear that it was completely and utterly pointless.

"Do you trust me?" he asked.

She hesitated for a brief second before nodding. "Yes, I trust you, Darien."

Cupping her cheeks, he leaned in and kissed her. Not a quick peck of lips but a long, thorough tasting of her. He needed her to know that he cared for her, that he would do whatever he could to free her from this curse.

He hugged her close and buried his face into the silk of her hair. "I'll get us out of here. I promise you."

Chapter 11

Twenty minutes later, Darien was outfitted for the blistering cold outdoors. He had the grappling hook and rope wrapped around his shoulder, ready to go. In the large hiking pack he put on his back, he shoved the rest of his stuff—a hot plate, thermal blanket and the small pup tent designed for extreme temperatures that Jiro had given to him.

Beside him, Koori stood only dressed in her kimono staring up at the ceiling. She told him she was impervious to the cold temperature and didn't need the extra clothing and equipment. She didn't even want or need shoes. He definitely would need everything he could carry, once they reached the outdoors.

As she surveyed the roof, he could see in her face that

she was just waiting for it to disappear. She'd shared with him the different ways she'd tried to escape and all of them had failed miserably with the palace reconstructing itself.

He glanced at the gaping hole and hoped it was too much damage for the castle to heal itself. He guessed they'd soon find out.

Holding the hook in one hand, he swung his arm up toward the break. The hook soared through the air, the rope trailing behind it like a kite's tail. Darien held his breath, praying as the hook disappeared through the gap. In seconds he was pulling on the rope. He could feel the hook move until finally, thankfully, it found purchase and stuck. He yanked on the rope again. It held firm.

"I'm going to go first and make sure it's safe up top."

Koori nodded and watched as he grabbed the rope in both hands and started to climb. The ceilings were high in the palace, so it took him a bit to make it to the top. Once there, he swung his leg up and onto the jagged ledge and pulled himself up. The ice didn't break. It held under his weight.

Leaning over the edge, he called down to Koori. "It's your turn. Grab the rope, and climb up to my hand." He held it out to show her she didn't have to climb that far to reach him.

Without hesitation, she gripped the rope and made her way up. She was strong, showing great power in both her arms and legs as she climbed hand over hand, bare feet clutching at the rope.

Six inches from reaching his outstretched hand, the ice started to reform.

By the way Koori's eyes widened in alarm she noticed it about the same time he did. "Darien!" she called, fear making her voice shrill.

"Keep coming! You can make it."

With every inch she advanced up the rope, the ice made the same progress. Darien watched in horror as it knitted back together faster than he could see. The sound was deafening, like a knife being sharpened faster and faster on a flint.

Wrapping his hand in the rope near the hook, Darien leaned farther into the hole stretching his fingers out to her. A long, agonizing minute later, she reached him.

Once they hooked fingers, he started to pull her up. Thankfully she weighed next to nothing, and progress was quick. But not as quick as the sheet of ice forming over the hole. It was going to be tight.

"Oh, God, Darien!"

He had her hand now firmly in his, now her arm, her head. Her shoulders came through, and he wrapped his hands around her waist to yank her body the rest of the way out. But the ice was forming too quickly. He wasn't strong or fast enough to save her. Her legs were going to be stuck in between. What would happen then? Would she be half in and half out of the palace for an eternity? He couldn't let that happen. He wouldn't.

With all his power, he yanked her up. Falling backward, he pulled her with him until finally she was through, the ice skimming her toes. The hole sealed shut with a final earsplitting shrill.

Darien lay on his back, breathing hard, Koori clutched to his chest. His arms were cramping, but he was afraid to let her go. Adrenaline still shot through his system, but it was starting to slow. He could hear her ragged breathing and knew she was struggling, too. It had been close. Too close for his heart to take.

Finally, she stirred against him. "You can let go now, Darien. I'm safe." He released his hold on her and she rolled off him onto the roof. Rising to her knees, she looked down at him and caressed his cheek. "Are you hurt?"

Sitting up, he shook his head. "No. But that was much too close for my liking."

She smiled. "Mine, as well."

Darien took in their surroundings. The wind howled around them, swirling snow and bits of ice into their faces. He didn't know how Koori could be unaffected as he was already starting to feel the bite of the cold. But she was. She wasn't even shivering. Long strands of black hair swirled around her head like a dark cloud of silk, but other than that there was no indication that the weather bothered her at all.

Luckily they were on a flat part of the roof, but the rest of it was constructed with turrets and points. They would definitely need the grappling hook and rope to get to the ground. He hoped he brought enough rope or else this might all be just an exercise in futility and they wouldn't be going anywhere.

He stood to get a better picture of their situation.

The view didn't do much for his confidence in getting them out. All he could see was gray. Above them, below them. All around. The blowing snow didn't help, either. It was as if he were standing in the middle of a gray tornado, directly in the center with no sense of direction. Despair washed over him, draining him of all the hope he'd mustered before attempting this crazy escape. He was going to fail her.

Movement at his side startled him from his reverie. Koori stood beside him, her hand curled around his.

"You have done more for me than I could possibly imagine. More than I have been able to do for myself." She squeezed his hand tight. "We can make it out of here together. I can feel it. For the first time in a thousand years I have hope. It is because of you."

He met her gaze and saw there the strength he needed to move on. She believed in him. Koori made him feel invincible, as if he could take on the world and win.

"Okay. The first thing we need to do is get off this roof."

He twisted around looking for the best and safest way to make their descent. Gathering the hook and rope, Darien walked to the edge of the flat surface and looked down. There was another level below this one. It was flat like this one and appeared to be stable.

"How many levels are there in this place?"

Koori shook her head. "I don't know. I've only ever been on one level."

Darien looked down again. He couldn't remember ever seeing any staircases in the castle, especially during his search for Koori's room. He guessed there could've been stairs possibly tucked into obscure corners, but he wondered why he never ran across one. The castle was huge, but as far as he could tell it was all on one level. Obviously, the palace had a mind of its own and decided to grow a few floors to make it more difficult for them to leave.

"It's more trickery and magic. Junzo was always very good at punishing people." Her voice was filled with hopelessness. He hated to hear it. It tore at him.

Digging the hook into the ice until he thought it was secure, he tossed the twenty feet of rope over the edge. Thankfully it reached the next tier so they wouldn't have to jump too far.

Once Darien was sure the grapple was safe, he motioned for Koori to come ahead. "You go down first. I'll make sure the rope holds. When you reach the bottom give me a sign that everything's okay."

Koori made her way down without any problem. When she reached the end, she gave Darien the thumbs-up. He smiled at that.

After pulling the rope up, he tied his pack onto the end. But before he let it down the side of the wall, he took out a set of boot picks and handheld ice picks used for mountain climbing. After securing the rope again, he tossed it over the side and let out slack slowly to prevent dumping the pack onto the next level. He didn't want anything inside it to break apart unnecessarily.

When it reached the bottom, Koori untied it and gave him another thumbs-up. He pulled the rope up but this time he pulled the hook out of the ground and tossed the whole thing over the edge. He couldn't use it to go down. He had to climb down another way.

Sitting down near the edge, Darien strapped the ice picks to the toes of his boots. Once secure, he swung his legs over the edge of the roof and stuck two ice picks into the roof to hold on to. So far so good. Slowly and steadily he made his way down.

It wasn't the first time he'd climbed down ice cliffs. He'd done some spelunking at the Columbia Icefield in Alberta, Canada, and in Iceland. But the slick walls on the castle weren't exactly like the cliffs he'd climbed. Instead of a gradual descent and small mounds and bumps to find purchase and footholds on, it was a straight slide down to the bottom. And he didn't have an anchor rope. Falling and breaking his legs wasn't exactly the way he wanted to get to the next tier.

About halfway down the wind picked up. At first it didn't bother him, but eventually it became a problem. Violent gusts pushed and prodded him. It was as if it were a separate entity trying to yank him off the wall. Whipping at his coat and pants, Darien felt the cold taking hold. It wouldn't be long before his legs went numb from the constant battering of the bitter wind. His only chance at making it was to keep moving.

Foot, foot, hand, hand. Darien concentrated on every motion he made. One small slip and he'd fall. He glanced down to see Koori waiting anxiously for him at the bottom. He was far enough down that even if he did fall, he wouldn't break anything vital. At least he didn't think he would.

Another violent flurry blew up and whipped at him. Squeezing his eyes shut against the barrage, Darien stilled and flattened his body against the icy wall. He could feel the wind racing over him as if trying to find a way to tear him away from the wall. Over and over it swirled around him until he could hear nothing but the strident cry of it.

He couldn't let it stop him. He had to make it down. He had to save Koori. That's all that mattered to him now. Gathering his strength, Darien started to move again, putting one foot down after another, using one handhold he made with the pick to the next. Methodical. Determined. Another few steps, and he finally set his foot down on the level roof.

Koori rushed to him, wrapping her arms around him. "I thought you were going to fall."

He hugged her close. "For a second there, so did I."

"What now?"

"Now, we go to the next level." Holding Koori's hand, Darien walked to the edge of the roof and looked down. He still couldn't see the ground. But he did see the next flat rooftop. It was another twenty feet down.

Glancing up into the sky, he wondered when night was going to fall. Doing this was dangerous enough in the murky gray light of the day; he couldn't imagine what it would be like in the absolute dark. He had a flashlight in his pack, but it wouldn't cast enough light to be helpful. One small slip and either of them could fall and get injured or worse. He hadn't come this far with Koori to fail. He just wouldn't.

"We need to hurry. Night is coming." And with that, he hooked the grapple into the ice and tossed the rope over. It was going to be a long day.

Chapter 12

Another three hours and they finally reached the ground. Koori sent up a silent prayer that they had made it right before full dark. The last leg of the descent had been treacherous at best in the waning light. Darien had slipped once, nearly falling the last ten feet and she had, too. The palms of her hands still ached from the rope burn.

Because they had no idea where they were, Darien didn't want to wander in the dark, so he had pitched a small tent at the base of the palace out of the worst of the wind. Inside the nylon hut it was surprisingly cozy and warm, but cramped. They had to lie down side by side. There wasn't much room to sit up. They drank water and ate the freeze-dried food Darien had in his pack.

They weren't ideal conditions but at least Koori felt

like they had a fighting chance to escape. Hope warmed her heart. And that was something she hadn't allowed herself in so long she could hardly remember what it actually felt like.

Darien handed her the canteen of water so she could wash down the barely edible food bar that she'd been chewing for the past ten minutes. She took a long drink and handed it back to him.

He glanced at his own bar and shrugged. "Hey, it's vitamins and energy that we'll need." He bit off another piece and chewed. After he swallowed, he said, "Once we're out of here I'll take you to the best restaurant in Tokyo."

She smiled, touched that he made the offer. "I've never been to Tokyo."

"Really? Well, let me tell you, it is something to see." He smiled. "Mind you, it's changed some in the past millennium."

"Yes, I imagine it has." Her smile faded.

She hadn't considered what it would be like for her if she ever got free. She couldn't even picture what the world would look like. Over the years, she had glimpses of some changes with every stranded stranger she came across. She could discern some things by the way they dressed or what vehicle they had driven. But she never let herself wonder for too long. It was too painful to think about. But now because of Darien, it was a possibility.

"What is your home like?" she asked.

He took another swig of water then capped the canteen and set it to the side. "It's a small town in

Montana. A place where everybody knows everybody whether you want them to or not." He smiled. "There're lots of trees and a small stream that runs just on the edge of my family farm. I'd go swimming in that stream every summer as a kid."

"I wish I could remember summer. I can't even remember the sun."

Darien set his hand over hers, linking their fingers together. "When we get out of here, I'll take you to that stream, and we'll go swimming in the hot summer sun."

"You would take me to your family home?"

"Yes." He squeezed her hand tight. "I'll take you wherever you want to go for however long you want to."

She didn't know what to say to that. She was overwhelmed with emotion. Emotions she hadn't experienced in so long that her heart throbbed with the intensity of everything. Here was this man, a man she had plucked out of his world and into hers, risking himself for her, to free her from this curse and offering more of his life and his time to her.

A tear slipped from her eye and she hurried to wipe it away before he saw it. But he beat her to it and brushed her cheek with his thumb. That was the second time he'd wiped her tears away. She didn't deserve such a sweet and caring man like Darien. There was so much about him that reminded her of Shiro, her lost lover, but there was a lot that was different. Where Shiro was feckless and unmotivated, Darien was strong and determined and spirited. She felt safe and protected with him. And the way he looked at her made her stomach clench and her thighs tingle with pleasure.

Exactly in the way he was looking at her now.

She lowered her gaze, aware that the temperature in the tent was rising. But she lifted her eyes again when he brushed the stray hairs from her face with the tips of his fingers. The touch sent shivers from the top of her head to the bottom of her feet.

"I don't know what it is about you," he sighed. "But every time I look at you my heart aches just a little bit more."

Smiling, she nuzzled against his palm as he cupped her cheek. Slowly, he stroked his thumb over her mouth. On a sigh, she parted her lips and pressed her tongue against his skin.

His eyes darkened to flint and she found she could hardly breathe as he leaned toward her mouth. It was torture waiting for his lips to touch hers, but when they did she felt a surge of fire between her legs.

The kiss was slow and liquid like melted honey in her mouth. Koori thought she would never taste anything as delectable as Darien's kiss. Not even the sweet taste of sugar could compare.

She moved her hands into the suppleness of his hair and deepened the kiss, pressing her tongue against his. As he moved his hands over the bodice of her kimono, she quivered under his touch. Her breasts ached for his caresses; her nipples peaked and throbbed in desperate need.

Darien slowly untied the ribbon at the side of her

garment. She groaned against his mouth, begging him to hurry. Soon it was undone and the fabric loosened, affording ample room for him to maneuver.

Koori moaned and arched her back as he captured her breast in the palm of his hand. The heat of his skin against hers sent waves of rapture over her body. She needed more, wanted his flesh pressed to her, to feel his hunger.

"Oh, please hurry, Darien."

He licked her earlobe and whispered into her ear. "I have thought of this moment too many times today to rush it away."

He watched her face as he pulled the top of her kimono down over her breasts, exposing them to the cool night air. With just one finger, he traced the slope of her breasts, circling her nipple with every stroke. Bending down, he brushed his tongue over her flesh, flicking her nipples with the tip.

"Beautiful," he moaned before pulling a nipple into his mouth and rolling it between his teeth.

Koori cried out as bolts of pleasure surged over her and nestled deep in her sex. She instinctively spread her legs to quiet the aching, but the movement only made it grow more intense.

As he sucked at her breast, Darien moved his hand down her body to her leg. He gathered her skirt and pushed it up, revealing her long legs. Slowly, he trailed his fingers up the smooth line of her skin and circled them over the soft, sensitive flesh of her inner thigh.

Shivering with desire, she pushed her hips up, inviting him in, to touch, to feel how she ached for him.

He didn't need any more encouragement as his fingers found her wet and open for his touch. He growled low in his throat and she felt his jaw clench at her breast as he continued to lick her creamy flesh.

"You feel like heaven in my hand."

As he gently stroked her, Koori could feel her desire building deep within her belly. No man had excited her as Darien had. There was something about his quiet manner that drove her mad. She moaned as his fingers pressed into her.

"Darien!" she cried. "Take me now. I need you inside me."

He let his hand slide out from between her legs, and quickly shed his thermal shirt and pants. With one mighty yank, he pulled her kimono down her body and tossed it to their feet. He leaned over her, gazing at her, as if drinking in his fill of her naked form.

"You are the most enchanting woman I have ever known, Koori, my ice maiden."

She smiled up at him and let her gaze travel over his body. She took in his tousled golden hair, the dark of his eyes, the hard rippling muscles of his chest, down to the full length of his cock. He was perfect in every way to her.

Wrapping her hands around his neck, she rolled him over her, wrapping her legs around his waist, inviting him in.

He nestled between her legs and kissed her hard. As he moved his mouth over hers, Koori could feel the rigidness of his sex pressing against her. She pushed toward him as he inched himself into her slowly. She felt every glorious inch of him as he went deep within her, filling her up. They fit perfectly, she thought, like two pieces of the same sculpture.

Pushed up on his elbows, Darien stared down into her face while he cradled her head in his hands. She could feel him pulsing inside her like a second heartbeat. She moved against him, but he stilled her. She felt the thud of his heart against her chest. It was hard and fast and strong, and made her feel more alive than anything before.

His intensity scared her as well as filled her with passion. When he looked at her, it was as if he were staring through her and into her soul. She wondered what he saw there. Was it as black as Junzo had told her it was? Or was it as wholesome and pure as she hoped it to be?

Whatever he saw must've pleased him because he pressed his lips to hers and started to move inside her.

With each thrust of his hard length, Koori held on to him. She wrapped her arms around him and whimpered as he drove her up a massive rise then cried out with her as they tumbled down the other side in an explosion of need and pleasure. Koori felt it deep within the place inside her that had solidified into ice so long ago.

Sweat trickled down his forehead as he moved inside her with a relentless rhythm. He took her up, and then back down again and again, until all she could do was feel. Every nerve ending in her body fired at once, and she was bombarded with a kaleidoscope of sensory overload. She could no longer discern where she started and Darien ended. It was as if they had fused into one entity from the heat burning up both of them.

Wrapping his hands around her head, he buried his face in her neck and drove himself deep into her. She dug her nails into his back and held on as she spiraled out of control. A deep violent vibration exploded inside her belly and radiated out to every part of her body. She even felt it in the tips of her fingers and toes.

With one final moan, Darien came, crying out in his pleasure. "Koori."

When their bodies quieted, Darien rolled off her and snuggled her into his body from behind, curling around her. He kissed the back of her neck with a sigh. His whiskers tickled her skin, and she squirmed against him, finding a perfect groove to snuggle into.

Koori felt sore, tired and completely blissful as Darien wrapped his arms around her and pressed his lips to the back of her neck again. His heat warmed her, drugging her like too much sake. Soon, her eyes felt heavy, and she started to drift on the edge of sleep.

Darien stroked his thumbs over the hollow of her belly and whispered into her ear. "I think I'm falling in love with you."

But Koori pretended not to hear. She wasn't sure if she was ready to hope for that. It had been so long she wasn't sure she even knew how to love or how to accept it. For now, it was enough to know that Darien really cared and that she did, too.

To expect any more was a fool's journey.

Chapter 13

It was the shrieking howl of the wind that woke Darien from his idyllic dreamsleep. Blinking to adjust to the gloom in the tent, he finally focused on where he was. Face-to-face, legs tangled, with a still-sleeping Koori, he smiled to himself. At first he'd thought he'd been dreaming of her, but now he realized that she was by his side, she was a reality.

He watched her sleep, the gentle rise and fall of her chest, the way her lips pursed together in a perfect cupid bow. She was extraordinary in every way.

A sudden blast of wind startled him from his reverie. He rolled onto his back and stared up at the flapping roof of the tent. The gravity of the situation smothered him in a sudden rush. They had escaped the palace but were now outside in a blizzard with no idea at all where to go. He had a compass, but he had a distinct feeling it wasn't going to help him in the least. He didn't think knowing north from south was going to aid him here in this place. Because it was quite possible that this place wasn't even real.

The thought had crossed his mind on several occasions as they made their way down impossible walls of ice of an impossibly structured castle that had no business being four stories high. Again, the notion that he was dreaming crossed his mind.

I could very well be going nuts.

Koori stirred beside him. With a small satisfied sigh, she ran her hand over his chest. He glanced down and realized that he was still naked. Surprisingly he wasn't in the least bit cold.

She nuzzled along his side, the feel of her body stirring more than just his mind. She stretched and yawned. "Is it morning?"

"I think so."

Yawning again, she laid her head on him and pressed a kiss to his chest. "I've not slept so well in more years than I care to consider."

"Me, either." He wrapped an arm around her and held her close, nuzzling his face into her hair. She smelled like fresh clean rain. It was one of his favorite scents.

"Do you think it wrong if we just stayed here, like this forever?"

He smiled. He had just been thinking the same thing, except in his version they were doing more than just lying there. "No, but I think eventually we'd run out of food. I only have enough food bars to last a week."

He had said it in jest, but the seriousness of the situation hung in the air like a rancid odor. They had to get moving, or one or both of them would die. And his big money was definitely on his own demise. Koori was immune to the cold, but he wasn't. Already he could feel the bitter wind beginning to seep in through the zipper and flaps of the tent tainting the air with ice.

"We should get moving."

"Yes." She rolled off him and reached for her kimono that he had earlier tore off her and thrown into the corner.

While she dressed, he, too, busied himself with clothing. He pulled on his thermals, then his sweatshirt and khaki pants. Next came his wool socks and boots, then his jacket.

Before he slipped on his gloves and wool hat, he rolled up the sleeping bags and thin insulated mat and shoved them into his pack. He handed Koori the canteen of water and an energy bar.

She took it without comment. He hated that the business of getting to safety ruined the magic brimming between them. But if he didn't get them out of here, they'd never have another magical moment together again.

"I'm going to go check things outside." He unzipped the tent and crawled out. He also had a bursting bladder to take care of.

The harsh wind hit him full-on in the face before he had a chance to put up the fur hood on his jacket. It stung his cheeks instantly. Gazing around at the surroundings, Darien could make out a few things in the gray haze of blowing snow. There did seem to be a path, or what should've been a path, between some barren trees running alongside the palace. Maybe it led to the road. Or maybe it led to absolutely nowhere. Regardless, they had to find out. They couldn't stay where they were and survive.

After finishing his business, he crawled back into the tent. Koori was busy chewing on the food bar.

"I think I see a path through some trees. It goes to the east. Does that sound familiar?"

She shook her head. "I take a different path just about every time I'm required to return to the road. At least it never seems like the same way." She shrugged. "I'm sorry that I'm of no help."

"That's okay." He smiled at her, but the defeated look on her face compelled him to lean into her and brush his lips against hers. He cupped her face with his hands and kissed her again. "We will get out."

She gave him a small smile, and a nod, but he didn't think she was too convinced of his declaration. Truth be told, he wasn't much, either.

After about an hour of walking through the barren craggy trees, it became evident to Darien that it wasn't leading them to a road. In fact, he felt like they'd somehow been going in circles. His compass wasn't working worth a damn.

What he wouldn't give for a gas station nearby so he could ask directions.

Stopping, he glanced over at Koori. "Does any of this look familiar?"

"Maybe," she said looking around at the surroundings. "But it all looks the same. Everywhere there are trees and snow and gray sky. That's all there ever is."

Darien could hear the panic in her voice. He wrapped an arm around her and squeezed her close. She shivered under his embrace.

He stared down at her. "Are you cold?"

"Yes, a little." Her teeth were starting to chatter. Her eyes widened in surprise by the action. She clutched at him. "Why am I cold?"

"I don't know." He dug into his pack and came away with another thermal shirt, a pair of long thermal underwear, wool socks and a pair of runners that he had stashed. He handed them to her to put them on. "Maybe it means we're getting closer. Maybe you're starting to become mortal again."

As she slid the clothes on under her kimono she seemed cheered by the idea. But Darien wasn't so quick to applaud. This could just be another trick, another layer to Junzo's cruel punishment.

Once Koori was outfitted, he took her in from head to toe. His thermal wear swam on her, but she managed to roll the pant legs up a bit. The sleeves also hung over her hands but at least they would provide warmth and protection to her hands. He smiled; she looked like a little girl playing dress-up.

"Why do you laugh?"

"You look—" he chuckled "—interesting."

She looked down at herself and started to laugh. Darien hugged her to him, and pressed his cold lips to the top of her head. He held her as she laughed, never wanting to let go. It felt too damn good having her pressed against him, sharing a light moment. He imagined they could have more of these times when they finally escaped this nightmare.

Just as they broke apart and were going to continue on, the wind picked up. It had already been blowing; a mild gust at best, but now it swirled around them like an angry tornado. Snow and ice pelted them from all sides.

Darien gathered Koori close again, trying to block the worst of it with his body. But it didn't matter where they turned, the wind whipped at them. It was as if they had done some terrible deed and the wind was inflicting its bitter retribution down on them. In any case, it came at them like hell's fury and made no sign of ever letting up.

Darien dug the rolled up nylon tent out of his pack and prepared to set it up, so they could at least have some reprieve from the howling, brutal wind. But just as soon as he had it unraveled, silence enveloped them and the wind died instantaneously as if it never had existed to begin with.

Stunned, Darien looked around them eyeing the surroundings, preparing for anything. Something had changed, something that he wasn't too sure he was going to like much.

And then Koori pointed to the north through the thin spattering of trees. "Look."

He followed her line of motion and saw a huge white wall of ice. It had to have been at least twenty-five feet tall, maybe even more. It was hard to tell from his line of sight. Was it the palace? Did they get turned around and walk right back to where they'd started?

Koori moved toward it and, after stuffing the tent back into the pack and hefting the bag onto his back, Darien followed her lead. As they approached, he reconsidered his first notion. It definitely wasn't the palace wall. It was too high and too long. He looked down the length of it both ways. It appeared to have no end.

"What is it, do you think?" Koori asked as she placed her hand on the wall, sliding it back and forth.

"Your guess is as good as mine. But it's a roadblock, that's for sure."

But it was as if Koori hadn't heard him. Looking up at the wall with glassy eyes, she ran her hand along the slick surface. Mesmerized, she moved down the wall caressing its surface. Darien wondered why it had enthralled her. More magic?

"Darien," she called, stopping along the wall only about four feet away from him. "There's an entrance."

He moved down to where she stood. Indeed there was an entrance, a wide opening with an arch over top. Looking down the wall, a person would've easily missed it, as it was cleverly camouflaged against the generic white of the surroundings.

Clasping hands, Darien and Koori stepped through the opening and into what appeared to be some sort of labyrinth that stretched out like a giant octopus with unending arms. He'd seen one or two in his lifetime but nothing of this magnitude. The first path in front of them was a straight lane into what appeared to be the center. There he saw a huge structure that looked like a sculpture of a woman. Who the woman was he couldn't be sure, but he had a strong suspicion she was standing right beside him.

"It's beautiful."

Darien nodded. It was stunning, but it was also eerie. He didn't like the dread creeping over him, as if they'd stepped into a trap that was going to snap on them at any moment.

"We should keep moving." He glanced behind him at the entrance they had just passed through. "I don't like the feel of this place."

Dropping his hand, Koori took a few steps forward. "I feel like we're almost there. I don't know why, but I almost feel free." She glanced over her shoulder at him and smiled.

And that was the last he saw of her before the walls moved.

Chapter 14

"Darien!" Koori rushed forward, but it was too late. The thick wall of ice slid in front of her, effectively blocking her from him. Again she shouted, "Darien!"

She received no reply.

Turning, she decided to proceed to the center of the maze and wait for him. That was the most logical course of action. But after taking only two steps another wall moved, sliding in front of her and preventing her from reaching the center.

Now there was only one way to proceed and that was to her left. Just as, she assumed, the labyrinth wanted her to go.

She walked along the path, fingers trailing along the icy wall. Maybe she could sense the next time the walls were about to move again. Maybe she could outsmart it or outrun it. Or maybe she was just thoroughly trapped without a hope of ever escaping.

Despair nearly ripped her in half. Tears threatened to spill from her eyes. She wanted to crouch down on the ground and succumb to it. But instead she wiped at her eyes and continued putting one foot in front of the other. She wouldn't quit. Not now. Not after all she'd been through, and all that Darien had done for her. To quit would be to quit on him. And she couldn't do that. She still believed that he would be her savior.

She followed the path through the maze, turning right, and then left. Then she came to a T and didn't know which way to turn. If she turned left, maybe she could backtrack and find Darien, but if she turned right, maybe she could find the center and stay there until Darien found her, which she knew he would. She turned right, hope making her stride quicken.

As she walked each path, she tried to keep her thoughts positive. But it was difficult. Especially when she made a wrong turn at another T and ended up at a dead end. She had to retrace her steps back to the T and turn the other way. By the eleventh corner she thought that she'd gone in a complete circle.

Dismissing the defeatist thought, Koori continued on. Sooner or later she'd either come across the center or Darien. The maze couldn't possibly be that enormous.

After another series of turns and dead ends, she had to retrace her steps again. Her feet were starting to throb. Not only from the cold but from the continual walking back and forth. Darien's runners weren't the most comfortable footwear, and the wool socks kept rubbing. She predicted she probably had at least three blisters on each foot.

But she pressed on, walking down pathway after pathway, every single one looking exactly like the last. The only way she could tell if she'd already walked down it was by the footprints in the snow. Hours passed without a break in the complicated maze.

Stopping to rest, Koori pressed her hands against the frozen barrier. If only she could feel through it to the other side. Maybe right this second Darien was on the opposite side thinking about her, wondering when he'd see her again and how to get to her.

"Darien!" she called, desperation starting to take a grip on her. There was no call in return, only the sounds of her own ragged breathing echoed back to her ears.

Defeat weighed down on her. Fighting the tears, Koori leaned against the wall and took in some deep breaths. She had to stop and think if she was going to get out of this. She couldn't let her emotions run rampant. Usually a levelheaded woman, she still couldn't stop the rush of anger and hopelessness surging through her. What if she never got out again? By the way her body shivered, it wouldn't be long before she succumbed to the cold and died. She never thought it would ever happen. Her death. She'd been alive for over a thousand years without ever a hope of ending her torment. Over the years she had certainly thought about ending it herself, but she'd always considered suicide a coward's way out.

But maybe now the day had finally come. Maybe the whole time when she hoped that Darien would free her, this was truly the only outcome that could happen. Actually leaving this world and being with Darien could have never been a possibility. Maybe it would only be a fleeting thought, a wishful dream and nothing more.

With that final thought, she let the tears fall. Her back braced against the wall, she slid to the ground. Wrapping her arms around her knees, she let the anguish take over, and she wept. For the first time in a thousand years, she let Junzo's curse overpower her will.

Darien didn't know how long he'd been running along the various pathways, but he figured at least two hours had passed. Every turn he took that didn't lead him to the center of the maze just propelled him on faster and harder. He had to find Koori.

He had the pack with all the food, the water and the tent for warmth. She had nothing but the few clothes on her back. If she was changing like he suspected she was, she wouldn't last very long exposed to the cold. The only grateful thing was that they were inside the walls of the maze and not out in the brutal wind.

Using his compass, Darien tried to keep to the north. That was the direction in which he'd seen the sculpture. It was the center of the maze and he knew he needed to get there. Koori would've thought the same. She might already be there waiting for him.

That thought spurred him on. Turn after turn he maneuvered through the labyrinth, his heart racing with anxiety. He couldn't believe they'd come this far to be thwarted by a maze made out of ice. Yes, it moved with a seeming life of its own, but it wasn't going to stop him from finding her.

Determined, Darien started to jog down the next path, taking one turn, then another. With his last turn, he stumbled out into an open clearing. He'd made it to the center.

"Koori," he called as he moved toward the middle, his gaze searching every crevice and entrance into and out of the maze. He didn't see her anywhere.

He kept walking until he was standing in the middle looking up at the twelve-foot sculpture crafted from blue ice on a crystal pedestal. It was indeed a woman, and there was no mistaking her dainty features and fierce gaze. The resemblance was uncanny. It was Koori larger than life, dressed in her kimono with her beautiful hair up in a complicated knot on top of her head, pinned there with the traditional Japanese hairpins.

Her frozen gaze peered over the tops of the maze toward the east. Darien wondered if she looked toward the way out, searching for her freedom. Or back toward the palace that had held her prisoner for so long.

As he looked up at the sculpture of Koori, he realized just how tied to the ice and to this place she truly was. Her cold skin, the rumblings in the palace, the breaking of the walls and ceiling right after they had made love. It all made sense to him now, in a strange, mystic way.

Every time he had touched her, the palace had shaken in response. When they had made love and he felt the heat of her body within, so the ice that made up the walls and ceiling had broken apart. As if she *was* the palace. Slowly, Darien had been thawing her out with every caress, every kind thought and every emotion.

Koori had been cursed with a heart of ice. And Darien had been the first man ever to find his way through the frozen layers.

Reaching out, he laid his hand on top of her frozen foot aching to be able to touch the real thing.

"Darien!"

He turned toward her voice. Smiling, she was running down one of the last paths heading toward the center, her hair an ebony cloud, his clothes hanging off her small frame. Setting his pack down, he rushed to meet her, anxious to have her safe in his arms again.

But as he walked he heard a soft rumbling that reminded him of the noise a mountain makes before an avalanche.

The walls were going to move again, effectively shutting them off from each other. He could feel it in his bones.

"Run faster!" he yelled as he charged ahead.

Eyes widening in alarm, Koori sprinted toward him. He was at the maze entrance when he saw the wall to her right begin to move. She was still five feet away from him. If either of them got in the way of the wall, it would crush them to death; he had no doubt in his mind.

With a loud whoosh, the wall slid forward, aiming right at them. It was going to be close.

He reached for her. She reached for him. Their

fingers brushed, and finally Darien was able to grab her hand and pull her forward.

Taking in a deep breath, Darien yanked Koori to his chest, wrapped her in his arms and swiveled to the right. They fell to the ground in a heap, barely out of harm's way. The wall smashed shut mere inches from Darien's feet. He could feel the sonic impact even through the hard rubber soles of his insulated boots.

He ran a gloved hand over her head, trying to find her face. "Are you okay?"

Clutching at him, she turned her head and found his mouth. She pressed her lips to his chin and cheeks in a smattering of kisses. "Oh, God, I thought I'd never see you again."

Smiling, he held her face still in his hands. "I didn't find you only to lose you. I'll always come for you." He covered her mouth with his, angling her head to deepen the kiss.

As they hugged and kissed, Darien felt the ground move beneath him. And this time he didn't think it was his nerves shaking his body.

Chapter 15

Darien scrambled to his feet, pulling Koori with him. He kept his arm around her to keep her from falling. The ground moved again, and they stumbled to the side, still holding on to each other.

"I don't think this place is very happy that we're back together."

Holding hands, they ran to the pack. Darien scooped it up and they went to stand in the middle of the eye of the labyrinth, away from anything that could break apart and fall on them.

A riotous rumbling sounded from underground. Darien had never heard anything like it. It sounded like a groaning giant awakening from a long sleep. Again the ground shook, a little faster and little harder than before.

All around them, pieces of the maze's walls began to crack and crumble to the ground. Large chunks came sliding across the slick ground toward them. They had to skate out of the way several times or be hit in the ankles by pounds of ice.

"I'm scared, Darien."

He hugged Koori tighter. Fear gripped him, too, but he couldn't let her see it. He had to be strong for her. "We'll be okay. We just need to hang on a little longer."

As if trying to contradict his statement, a loud resonating crack rang out in the air, echoing off the icy walls. The sound made Darien's ears and jaw ache. From the corner of his eye, he saw the ice maiden statue rock back and forth on its pedestal as if someone were actually pushing it.

Koori turned then, nudging Darien's arm from her view and watched in horror as the sculpture with her face started to crack. At first, small crystalline pieces fell off. They tinkled like bells as they hit the ground one by one. The sound became louder, harsher, as they fell in larger chunks and in mass quantities.

She struggled in his arms, as if she wanted to rush to her icy self's aid. But Darien kept her still. "Let it happen, Koori. When it's over we'll be free."

"Are you sure?"

He hesitated, and then said, "No, but I don't want you to get hurt."

She glanced at him, maybe searching his face for the truth or reassurance. He wasn't sure what she found when she looked but she finally settled back into his arms and didn't make another attempt to rush toward the crumbling statue.

Darien didn't know how long the ground kept shaking. It could've been a good half hour while the walls around them broke apart and the ice sculpture collapsed. They had fallen a couple of times because of the intensity of the tremors in the ground. But they had gotten back up, arms around each other and watched as everything around them fall apart.

Then it became quiet, and every single wall of the maze had been knocked down. For as far as he could see, there were jagged white pieces of ice sticking up haphazardly here and there. In some places, the wall had been completely obliterated. It appeared to go on for miles.

The ice sculpture of Koori was unrecognizable as ten thousand shards, chunks and pieces littered the area. Some had slid across the ground in an explosive array.

"Is it over?" Koori asked as she eyed the destruction around them.

Darien moved toward the ruined statue, kicking chunks of ice with the toes of his boots. "I think so."

"Do you think we'll be able to get out of here now?"

He heard the hesitancy in her voice. She wasn't convinced that it was over. To be honest, he wasn't sure, either. The wind had died down, the snow had stopped blowing. It even seemed a bit brighter out. All signs pointed to an end to something, but he couldn't be sure what that end meant.

"Well, the maze is destroyed so it should be straight walking to the road from here." *I hope.* He kept that last little bit to himself as he continued to circle the destroyed statue and pedestal.

"Darien?"

When he glanced at her, his chest tightened. Something was wrong. He could see it on her face.

"I feel different."

"How?"

She put a hand to her chest and frowned. "I don't know. Something inside me feels…strange. Warm, like the sensation I remember from the sun." She rubbed at her chest with the heel of her hand. Tears trickled down her cheeks.

Darien moved toward her, his hand outstretched. "It's okay, Koori. I think you're finally free of this place. I think you were actually part of this place and your heart was the last thing that needed to thaw."

She smiled through the tears and lifted her hand toward him. Before he could touch her fingers, the ground trembled again. But this time it sounded different.

The ground cracked open between them. Like a strike of lightning it zigzagged the length of the courtyard, pieces of the walls falling into the crevice.

Wobbling, Darien fell to his knees, unable to keep his footing. He watched in horror as Koori also fell to the ground, but she was also sliding toward the ever-expanding crater between them.

"Koori!" he yelled as he scrambled toward the gap in the ground.

Flailing her arms and legs, she couldn't stop from slipping on the ice toward the crack. She was heading feetfirst without the hint of slowing down.

Darien dove across the ground, sliding on his stomach with his arms outstretched as far as they could go. He had to catch her. He couldn't let her go. Not this way.

Screaming, she tumbled into the expanding fracture. Digging her fingers into the ice edge, she tried to stop her fall, but it was useless. Her nails broke off as she continued to slide down. Both runners on her feet slid off and tumbled into the dark gap.

Darien kept reaching for her.

Reaching.

Straining.

Darien caught her by the fingertips with one hand. Legs dangling in midair, Koori tried to keep still so she could get a better hold on him.

"Reach up, and grab my arm," he grunted, as he teetered on the edge of the crevice on his stomach. Luckily he had kept one of the ice picks in his jacket pocket and it was now jabbed into the ice and he was holding on to it with his other hand. It kept him anchored.

Koori stretched up with her other hand and gripped his forearm. Darien started to shuffle backward, drawing her with him.

"I'm slipping," she cried.

"I got you, darling. I got you." But the truth was he could feel his glove starting to slide off his hand. He just needed to get a little bit closer to the edge, so he could use his other hand to grab her. "Just a little bit farther. Hold on to me."

"Don't let go, Darien."

"I won't."

He kept her gaze as he continued to shimmy backward, pulling her with him. He saw the fear in the breathtaking pale depths but also something else, something that surprised him. He saw love. For him.

His heart throbbed, and his chest tightened even more. He could hardly breathe. He had to save her. He'd fallen in love with her, and now she was going to be taken from him.

"We're almost there, Koori. I won't let you fall."

He glanced over his shoulder to see how far he was. Just another few inches, and he'd be stable enough to use his other hand without the threat of falling in face-first.

"Darien?"

When he looked back at her, she slipped a bit from his hold. Tears streaked her pale cheeks, but gone was the fear in her eyes. Resignation had replaced it. She was barely gripping his gloved hand.

Fear made him readjust his grip. But when he turned his arm, there was a sickening, aching popping sound as his shoulder joint popped out of its socket.

Pain tore through him like wildfire. Tears welled in his eyes and he had to swallow down the bile that rose in his throat. Blinking back the tears, he bit down on his lip to push back the pain. He'd been through worse. He tried to remember the time he'd broken his arm skiing. The pain had been worse. He managed to get through that.

"Don't forget me," she whispered.

"You're not going anywhere." Just one more inch. Just one more. *Hang on.*

"It's okay. You can let go."

He shook his head. He was almost there. "I won't."

She smiled up at him. "I've fallen in love with you. You thawed this ice maiden out. My heart belongs to you forever."

"Koori!" he cried. "No!"

But it was too late. His glove gave, and she fell.

Unable to breathe, Darien reached for her. Letting himself slide down the ice, he tried to grab her. His fingers brushed hers, but that was it. He couldn't get a grip on her hand.

He released his hold on the ice pick and dove in after her.

Chapter 16

He was falling.

Darkness swallowed him. He couldn't see anything or feel anything around him. It was as if he were floating in the air. Although he felt no wind on his face or in his hair. And the air always had a certain smell.

He couldn't smell anything now.

His stomach flipped over and over. Doing somersaults in his gut. He had dove into the crevice to save Koori. So he had to be falling.

Wasn't he?

Reaching out with his arms, Darien grasped for something, anything to stop his fall. But his hands came up empty. There was nothing there to grasp. The crater hadn't been that deep, had it?

The pain was even gone. He couldn't feel the ripping agony searing him from his dislocated shoulder. He still should be in pain. It should be tearing through him like an angry grizzly bear with his next meal.

A sense of extreme loss surged through him. Something was deathly wrong.

"Koori!" he shouted.

No response. Even his voice didn't echo back to him.

It felt like he was in a vacuum. No air, no sound, no smell, no sight. When he thought about it, he couldn't really feel himself, either.

He thought he was moving his hand, wanted it to touch his shoulder. But he had no sensation of actually moving and no feeling of touch. What was happening?

"Koori!" he shouted again. But did his mouth actually move? Or was he just thinking of her name?

Tears welled in his eyes, but he didn't feel them on his face. He couldn't feel anything, not physically anyway.

But mentally, he was in agony.

Was he dead? Was this what death felt like? An empty sensation-free vacuum? Where was the bright light? Where were the singing angels welcoming him to the heavenly gates?

There was no heaven, he thought. There couldn't be without Koori.

Sinking into himself, Darien tried to shut it all down. Tried to turn off the emotions raging through him. He wanted to wrap his arms around himself, but knew he'd never feel it, anyway. So he tried to do that inside his mind.

But that was when he saw the light.

At first it was only a white pinprick, hardly anything to discern. Regardless, he felt his mind rushing toward it in desperation. If this was the way to end his torment, then he'd do it. He'd run to the light.

The light grew in scope and in hue. Sound hummed in his ears. A strong stringent odor erupted in his nostrils. Physical sensations began to prickle across his arms and hands. Like pins and needles they tingled across his body.

It was too much. It was sensory overload and it felt like his brain was going to explode. Pain pounded at his temples, and he cried out.

"Mr. Calder?"

The voice nearly burst his eardrums. He shook his head from side to side to dislodge the painful ringing in his ears.

There was pressure against his temples and his forehead.

"Mr. Calder? Can you hear me?"

The light was too bright. It was going to blind him. He tried to close his eyelids, but something pried them open. Panicked, he tried to lift his hands to cover his face. But he found he couldn't move them.

"Someone help me!" he shouted. His voice pinged in his ears.

"I am here to help, Mr. Calder." More pressure on his head. "You have to calm down."

There was something in the man's accented voice that gave Darien pause. He'd heard that kind of tone before. It was the voice of someone used to being in charge, used to being listened to.

Calming his breathing, he tried to relax. He stopped fighting the pressure on his eyes and his head. When he did that, some of the discomfort abated. Blinking several times, his vision cleared, and he could see someone leaning into his line of sight.

It was a Japanese man with glasses. He was holding a thin penlight in one hand; his other hand was on Darien's forehead.

"Can you see me, Mr. Calder?" the man asked.

Darien nodded.

"I am Dr. Iwasaki."

Realization flooded Darien like a tsunami. Turning his head, he looked around. He was in a small area with a faded green curtain cutting him off from the rest of the white-walled room. Machines beeped beside him. An IV was stuck in his hand, the pole next to his bed, the water bag hanging from a cord.

He was in a hospital.

Darien licked his lips. They were cracked and sore. "Where—" his throat hurt bad; he tried again "—where am I?"

"You are in Sapporo City Hospital."

He licked his lips again. The doctor brought a plastic cup with a straw sticking out of it to his mouth.

"Drink."

Darien took a couple of sips of water. His throat had felt like it'd been torn into by large sharp claws. The cool liquid instantly soothed the ache.

The doctor set the cup on the swinging tray attached to his bed. "Take it slowly."

"How…"

"You were flown here from Kushiro three days ago."

Panic started to take root. Reality was closing in on him, and he didn't want to face it. He struggled to sit up, but the doctor held him still.

"You must rest. You do not suffer from any life-threatening injuries now, but you must stay still and rest. You came in with a dislocated shoulder and severe frostbite in some of your extremities. You were in the early stages of hypothermia. If you'd been found any later, I do not think you would have made it." He shook his head. "I am surprised because according to Jiro, your scientist friend, you have been missing for over a week. Seven days out in that cold and snow without shelter, food and water, you should technically be dead."

Darien didn't want to hear it. The doctor had to be wrong.

Craning his neck, he looked over to his right hand where the IV had been deposited. The tips of two of his fingers were black like he'd dipped them in ink. He tried to wriggle his feet and imagined the same type of effects on his toes.

The doctor patted him on his good shoulder. "You rest. I will be back to see you later. The nurse will be in to take your vitals and give you some food." He turned to leave, then said, "Oh, and someone from your embassy will also be by to see you." With that, he disappeared behind the flimsy green curtain, leaving Darien with only his despair for comfort.

He could feel it welling up inside him, drowning

his heart in the agony. Clamping his eyes shut, he tried to keep it back, tried to ignore the reality of his situation. He shook his head. He didn't want to believe it. He couldn't and survive. The pain would be too much.

Behind his eyes, an image of Koori took root. She was smiling, her eyes swimming with love for him. She was real. He could still smell her; still feel her on the tips of his fingers. She'd been real. As real as the bed beneath his body was real or the IV sticking in his veins.

He had not dreamed the past few days. It hadn't been a hallucination while he'd been in and out of consciousness, nearly frozen on the side of the road to Kushiro.

His heart panged, and he had to gasp to get a breath. Pain ripped through him, clawing at his insides, ripping at his soul. He brought a hand up to his chest and rubbed at his sternum. He'd never felt agony like that before. Not after falls off mountains or a plethora of broken limbs.

This was pain he didn't think he could ever heal.

Tears slipped from his eyes and rolled down his temples to drip onto the pillow. The agony of what he'd lost couldn't compare to any of his physical injuries. Those would eventually heal in time. This pain, this suffering, how could it ever be fixed?

The curtain fluttered open, and the nurse came in. She was an older woman, petite and quiet, unassuming in her manner as she set a tray of food on the swivel tray.

Darien ignored her as she took his temperature and blood pressure. She then listened to his heartbeat. He didn't care whether that organ ever beat again. It was broken, anyway. What good was it now? The doctor might as well cut it out of him. It was frostbitten just like his fingers and toes.

When she was checking him out, she pushed the tray forward. "You eat."

Darien ignored her, his face turned away from her. He didn't want her to see his pain. She couldn't help him with it.

Before she left, she patted him on the leg. "Girlfriend is here. She help you eat." She then disappeared through the curtain.

Darien turned toward the still-fluttering curtain. Girlfriend? He didn't have one, unless Jessica decided that she still cared for him and flew all the way to Japan to see him. Highly unlikely.

The curtain swished aside. All his breath left him in one powerful whoosh. How could it be?

"Hello, Darien." She smiled that little smile of hers and he felt as if he was falling all over again.

Koori. She was real.

As she moved into the cubicle, he noticed she was wearing jeans and a deep-green V-neck sweater that hugged her curves. Her hair was unbound, cascading over her shoulders and around her pale neck like ebony waves. He'd never seen anyone more beautiful than her.

She slid a hip up onto his bed and touched his arm. The heat from her fingertips warmed every part of his body. Especially his heart. It began to beat again, as if waking from a deep sleep.

"How are you feeling?"

He opened and closed his mouth unable to form any coherent words. He shook his head.

"You're going to be okay. The doctor says you won't lose any of your fingers or toes." She caressed each of his blackened digits. "They just look bad."

He turned his hand over and caught her fingers in his. The weight and heat of her touch made him ache. "Are you real?"

She smiled. "Yes, Darien. I'm real. I'm here, sitting at your side."

"I'm not going to wake up from a dream and you'll be gone forever?"

She shook her head and squeezed his hand tightly to show him how very real she was. "I'm not going anywhere. I'm staying right here with you."

"I saw you fall."

"We both fell."

"I don't understand. How are we not both dead?"

"The crack in the ground was the way out, Darien. It was the slip between our worlds. When we fell through, we both landed not far from the main road."

"Why don't I remember it?"

She lifted his hand up to her mouth and pressed her lips to the back. Her touch was warm, not the cold press he remembered.

"You hit your head during the fall. When we arrived at the road, you were unconscious. The storm had stopped, so I was able to pitch the tent around you for heat, and I ran to the road and flagged down help."

"We're out."

She nodded, her lovely mouth lifting at the corners. "You're free?"

"Yes, Darien, I'm free, all because of you." She shuffled closer to him and leaned down to his face. She pressed a soft kiss to his cheek and murmured against his skin, "You lifted the curse from me. You saved my life."

"And you saved mine," he whispered back.

She sat back up and ran her fingers over his cheek, jaw and finally down to his chest. She placed her palm over his heart. "Do you hurt anywhere?"

He shook his head and covered her hand with his. "Not anymore."

A single tear rolled down her cheek and dripped onto their covered hands. It was warm and real and the most perfect thing he'd ever felt.

"Come here." He motioned with his chin for her to bend down.

She did, moving slowly, a small smile on her lips. And when she was the barest of breaths away from his mouth, he whispered, "I'm yours forever."

And then he kissed her.

* * * * *

Here is a sneak preview of
A STONE CREEK CHRISTMAS,
the latest in Linda Lael Miller's acclaimed
McKETTRICK *series.*

A lonely horse brought vet Olivia O'Ballivan to
Tanner Quinn's farm, but it's the rancher's love
that might cause her to stay.

A STONE CREEK CHRISTMAS
Available December 2008
from Silhouette Special Edition.

Tanner heard the rig roll in around sunset. Smiling, he wandered to the window. Watched as Olivia O'Ballivan climbed out of her Suburban, flung one defiant glance toward the house and started for the barn, the golden retriever trotting along behind her.

Taking his coat and hat down from the peg next to the back door, he put them on and went outside. He was used to being alone, even liked it, but keeping company with Doc O'Ballivan, bristly though she sometimes was, would provide a welcome diversion.

He gave her time to reach the horse Butterpie's stall, then walked into the barn.

The golden retriever came to greet him, all wagging

tail and melting brown eyes, and he bent to stroke her soft, sturdy back. "Hey, there, dog," he said.

Sure enough, Olivia was in the stall, brushing Butterpie down and talking to her in a soft, soothing voice that touched something private inside Tanner and made him want to turn on one heel and beat it back to the house.

He'd be damned if he'd do it, though.

This was *his* ranch, *his* barn. Well-intentioned as she was, *Olivia* was the trespasser here, not him.

"She's still very upset," Olivia told him, without turning to look at him or slowing down with the brush.

Shiloh, always an easy horse to get along with, stood contentedly in his own stall, munching away on the feed Tanner had given him earlier. Butterpie, he noted, hadn't touched her supper as far as he could tell.

"Do you know anything at all about horses, Mr. Quinn?" Olivia asked.

He leaned against the stall door, the way he had the day before, and grinned. He'd practically been raised on horseback; he and Tessa had grown up on their grandmother's farm in the Texas hill country, after their folks divorced and went their separate ways, both of them too busy to bother with a couple of kids. "A few things," he said. "And I mean to call you Olivia, so you might as well return the favor and address me by my first name."

He watched as she took that in, dealt with it, decided on an approach. He'd have to wait and see what that turned out to be, but he didn't mind. It was a pleasure just watching Olivia O'Ballivan grooming a horse.

"All right, *Tanner,*" she said. "This barn is a disgrace.

When are you going to have the roof fixed? If it snows again, the hay will get wet and probably mold…"

He chuckled, shifted a little. He'd have a crew out there the following Monday morning to replace the roof and shore up the walls—he'd made the arrangements over a week before—but he felt no particular compunction to explain that. He was enjoying her ire too much; it made her color rise and her hair fly when she turned her head, and the faster breathing made her perfect breasts go up and down in an enticing rhythm. "What makes you so sure I'm a greenhorn?" he asked mildly, still leaning on the gate.

At last she looked straight at him, but she didn't move from Butterpie's side. "Your hat, your boots—that fancy red truck you drive. I'll bet it's customized."

Tanner grinned. Adjusted his hat. "Are you telling me real cowboys don't drive red trucks?"

"There are lots of trucks around here," she said. "Some of them are red, and some of them are new. And *all* of them are splattered with mud or manure or both."

"Maybe I ought to put in a car wash, then," he teased. "Sounds like there's a market for one. Might be a good investment."

She softened, though not significantly, and spared him a cautious half smile, full of questions she probably wouldn't ask. "There's a good car wash in Indian Rock," she informed him. "People go there. It's only forty miles."

"Oh," he said with just a hint of mockery. "*Only* forty miles. Well, then. Guess I'd better dirty up my truck if I want to be taken seriously in these here parts. Scuff up my boots a bit, too, and maybe stomp on my hat a couple of times."

Her cheeks went a fetching shade of pink. "You are twisting what I said," she told him, brushing Butterpie again, her touch gentle but sure. "I meant…"

Tanner envied that little horse. Wished he had a furry hide, so he'd need brushing, too.

"You *meant* that I'm not a real cowboy," he said. "And you could be right. I've spent a lot of time on construction sites over the last few years, or in meetings where a hat and boots wouldn't be appropriate. Instead of digging out my old gear, once I decided to take this job, I just bought new."

"I bet you don't even *have* any old gear," she challenged, but she was smiling, albeit cautiously, as though she might withdraw into a disapproving frown at any second.

He took off his hat, extended it to her. "Here," he teased. "Rub that around in the muck until it suits you."

She laughed, and the sound—well, it caused a powerful and wholly unexpected shift inside him. Scared the hell out of him and, paradoxically, made him yearn to hear it again.

* * * * *

Discover how this rugged rancher's wanderlust is tamed in time for a merry Christmas, in
A STONE CREEK CHRISTMAS.
In stores December 2008.

Silhouette

SPECIAL EDITION™

FROM *NEW YORK TIMES* BESTSELLING AUTHOR

LINDA LAEL MILLER

A STONE CREEK CHRISTMAS

Veterinarian Olivia O'Ballivan finds the animals in Stone Creek playing Cupid between her and Tanner Quinn. Even Tanner's daughter, Sophie, is eager to play matchmaker. With everyone conspiring against them and the holiday season fast approaching, Tanner and Olivia may just get everything they want for Christmas after all!

Available December 2008
wherever books are sold.

MIRA®

The chilling
Flynn Brothers trilogy
from bestselling author

HEATHER GRAHAM

SAVE $1.⁰⁰

DEADLY NIGHT
DEADLY HARVEST
DEADLY GIFT

Coming October 2008.

SAVE $1.⁰⁰ on the purchase price of one
book in the Flynn Brothers trilogy
by Heather Graham.

Offer valid from September 30, 2008, to December 31, 2008.
Redeemable at participating retail outlets. Limit one coupon per purchase.
Valid in the U.S. and Canada only.

52608517

Canadian Retailers: Harlequin Enterprises Limited will pay the face value of this coupon plus 10.25¢ if submitted by customer for this product only. Any other use constitutes fraud. Coupon is nonassignable. Void if taxed, prohibited or restricted by law. Consumer must pay any government taxes. Void if copied. Nielsen Clearing House ("NCH") customers submit coupons and proof of sales to Harlequin Enterprises Limited, P.O. Box 3000, Saint John, NB E2L 4L3, Canada. Non-NCH retailer—for reimbursement submit coupons and proof of sales directly to Harlequin Enterprises Limited, Retail Marketing Department, 225 Duncan Mill Rd., Don Mills, Ontario M3B 3K9, Canada.

U.S. Retailers: Harlequin Enterprises Limited will pay the face value of this coupon plus 8¢ if submitted by customer for this product only. Any other use constitutes fraud. Coupon is nonassignable. Void if taxed, prohibited or restricted by law. Consumer must pay any government taxes. Void if copied. For reimbursement submit coupons and proof of sales directly to Harlequin Enterprises Limited, P.O. Box 880478, El Paso, TX 88588-0478, U.S.A. Cash value 1/100 cents.

5 65373 00076 2   (8100) 0 11566

® and TM are trademarks owned and used by the trademark owner and/or its licensee.
© 2008 Harlequin Enterprises Limited

MHGTRI08CPN

REQUEST YOUR FREE BOOKS!

2 FREE NOVELS PLUS 2 FREE GIFTS!

Silhouette®

nocturne™

Dramatic and Sensual Tales of Paranormal Romance.

YES! Please send me 2 FREE Silhouette® Nocturne™ novels and my 2 FREE gifts (gifts are worth about $10). After receiving them, if I don't wish to receive any more books, I can return the shipping statement marked "cancel." If I don't cancel, I will receive 4 brand-new novels every other month and be billed just $4.47 per book in the U.S. or $4.99 per book in Canada, plus 25¢ shipping and handling per book plus applicable taxes, if any*. That's a savings of about 15% off the cover price! I understand that accepting the 2 free books and gifts places me under no obligation to buy anything. I can always return a shipment and cancel at any time. Even if I never buy another book from Silhouette, the two free books and gifts are mine to keep forever.

238 SDN ELS4   338 SDN ELXG

Name _____ (PLEASE PRINT) _____

Address _____ Apt. # _____

City _____ State/Prov. _____ Zip/Postal Code _____

Signature (if under 18, a parent or guardian must sign) _____

Mail to the Silhouette Reader Service:
IN U.S.A.: P.O. Box 1867, Buffalo, NY 14240-1867
IN CANADA: P.O. Box 609, Fort Erie, Ontario L2A 5X3

Not valid to current subscribers of Silhouette Nocturne books.

Want to try two free books from another line?
Call 1-800-873-8635 or visit www.morefreebooks.com.

* Terms and prices subject to change without notice. N.Y. residents add applicable sales tax. Canadian residents will be charged applicable provincial taxes and GST. Offer not valid in Quebec. This offer is limited to one order per household. All orders subject to approval. Credit or debit balances in a customer's account(s) may be offset by any other outstanding balance owed by or to the customer. Please allow 4 to 6 weeks for delivery. Offer available while quantities last.

Your Privacy: Silhouette is committed to protecting your privacy. Our Privacy Policy is available online at www.eHarlequin.com or upon request from the Reader Service. From time to time we make our lists of customers available to reputable third parties who may have a product or service of interest to you. If you would prefer we not share your name and address, please check here. ☐

SN08R

nocturne™

COMING NEXT MONTH

#53 SCIONS: REVELATION • Patrice Michelle
Scions

Emma Gray lives a secluded life until her aunt is captured
by the evil panther leader who wants to manipulate
Emma's powers and take over the entire panther pride.
Now, with the help of Caine Gerard—the mysterious man
she finds herself helplessly attracted to—Emma must
overcome the wicked leader and set the worlds of the
vampires, werewolves and panthers on their proper paths.

#54 HOLIDAY WITH A VAMPIRE II
Merline Lovelace and Lori Devoti

Ring in the holidays with two tales of paranormal
romance that uncover the true Christmas spirit. In
"A Christmas Kiss," Delilah Wentworth plans on spending
Christmas Eve at her clan's traditional vampire gathering.
But after a night that leaves her with an aching desire
for the affections of Sergeant Brett Cooper, a mortal who
thought he had given up on passion five Christmases ago,
they both realize that this love may be forbidden....

In "The Vampire Who Stole Christmas," vampire
Drystan Hurst is determined to seek revenge on his
adoptive mother on Christmas Eve, when all eyes will be
watching. The last thing he expects is to fall in love with
Aimee Polk, a key player in his plan of payback. Caught
between opposing emotions, can Drystan succumb to true
happiness?

SNCNMBPA1108